# The Island
# Ran Red

# The Island Ran Red

Michele M. Green

BLUEBERRY
LANE BOOKS

NEW YORK

Michelegreen.net
Blueberrylanebooks.com

Cover photo by Jay Fleming Photography
Cover design by Kevin Michaels

ISBN: 978-1-942183-13-6

*"Only a life lived for others is a life worthwhile."*

Albert Einstein

*The Island Ran Red* is an imaginary story based on my impression of a nonfictional existence on the water. Names and places are imaginary and are used solely to suit the author's fancy, except for my dogs Sara Jane and Bam Bam who cannot read.

-Michele M. Green

*-Prologue-*

"Grab the boat hook, Molly. It's probably just some grass tangled in the prop, damn scrape boats." Hank could tell something was off with the engine's mechanics just by listening to the motor's hum. The only thing I hear is the same complaint about the scrap nets digging up the eel grass year after year.

Not too worried by the sound, Hank continued sorting the crab trap's catch from the cull box, tossing varied stages of the peeler crabs into their colored-coded designated baskets.

"Where is it? I don't see the hook." I didn't know what hell he was talking about. Sometimes I feel so dim-witted and inadequate at this watermen's way of life. It feels foreign, as natural to me as boobs on a bullfrog.

"Look, it's right by your feet. Good thing it can't bite ya."

"Oh yeah, I see it now," I hollered over the engine noise, cautiously fetching the boat hook from the hull's sloshing dirty brown water, then turning off the grunting engine; at least I could remember to do that. The billowy eel grass swirled to the surface as I peeled the lime green blades, strand by strand from the prop. Hank would need to reach down into the water and grab the whole gobby mess.

"Can you pry it off by yourself or do you need me to come back there?" He grew agitated with my inability even though he knew I was leery to touch it.

"I dunno, maybe I can manage it."

"Cripes Molly, it's just some grass," he barked again.

"It's heavy; something else must be stuck in it. Wait, I think I have it now," I said yanking on the tangled chaos, managing only to spring loose a few more slimy splotches, splattering my face with salty green goo. Desperately pulling on the rod one last time, I was able to free the engine's prop from the slippery grass's grip.

"What is it? A crab pot buoy I bet," Hank asked, but I didn't answer him. I couldn't answer. I stood still, dazed with my mouth open, staring at the bloated pale white female torso floating before me, its breast nipples bobbing through the surface water. My stomach began to sway to the rhythm of the Southern Skimmer's slow rocking movement. I let the hook clank down to the deck bottom. My knees buckled. Grabbing hold of the rail, I hurled the contents of my breakfast over the side.

"Seriously Mol, I thought you would have gotten your sea legs by now." Hank ambled on back around the wooden bushel baskets towards the stern to look out past the engine. "Aw you know not," he gasped. "That ain't right. Nope, that's about as wrong as you can get."

My legs were as useful as rubber stilts. I couldn't turn my eyes away from the horror and watched as my husband reached out with the aluminum rod towards the torso, hooking the gaping severed neck wound and secured the body with a rope to the cleat before she drifted away. Unable to escape the putrid odors that choked the air, my vision faded slowly, losing sight of the woman's body before I fainted hard onto the boat's gel-coated deck.

**SIRENS WAILED ALONG** the water and up through my head, startling my puzzled aching mind into a semi cognitive state. "What the hell is going on, Hank? Why are my clothes wet?"

I sat up, looking over the side of the gunnel at the large numbers of official Marine Police boats which had surrounded the Tangier Sound, scouring the water with the Department of Natural Resource Police and Coastguard among them. Desperate garbled voices bounced across the swells communicating through their VHF radio, channel 16.

How long had I been unconscious? I couldn't understand what I was seeing. Many of the boats were marking areas with red and white buoys. It could well have been a flotilla celebration on the Fourth of July, and although I knew it wasn't, I couldn't understand what was happening.

I touched my wet hair embedded with fish goo. "Hank, what's going on? Why are there so many police boats?"

He was talking on his cell phone to Walter, the local sheriff and Hank's close friend. I couldn't make out everything he said. My hearing wasn't quite right and my head was beginning to throb. Maybe I whacked it when I fell down, and gave myself a concussion. The only thing familiar to me was the vibrations from the engine's pulsating drone as it crashed over the waves.

"Hank, tell me what is going on? Where are we?" There was an old towel from the console wrapped around my body. Hank must have covered me. I recognized the landscape—we were heading back home by the same daily route after running crab pots just like on any other day, except judging by the police escort that hovered by the crab boat's port side, today's catch wasn't like any other. It all seemed like a dream on a fast forward setting. I took a glimpse at the police boat's passenger and lost my air. No, this wasn't a dream after all. The black cadaver bag was a sobering reminder of what I'd seen; it held the remains of someone who once was alive. I began to shake from head to toe.

"This isn't real," I cried, covering my face. I closed my eyes and rocked my body, hoping this would make it all go away.

Several State Police squad cars, along with the Somerset County Coroner's Van were already perched, awaiting our return to the community pier, and standing alongside were the full-time residents of Smithtown, all nine of them. My mind grew as numb as my hands as we floated nearer to the bulkhead.

"It'll be alright Molly, you'll see." Hank briefly looked over his shoulder, uttering consoling words but I didn't pay attention to what he said. I was hypnotized and pulled by the whirling dome lights that danced playfully over the wharf with alternating colors of red and blue flashing onto the faces of my neighbors, underscoring the devastating truth crashing down on us all. A reality they knew as well as I did, one that would change our lives in Smithtown forever.

## - *One* -

A hard knock struck the front door triggered the dog alarm into a full-blown shrill. I was upstairs in the bedroom dressing after a hot shower. I couldn't get out of my wet clothes fast enough and put the morning behind me. I needed to forget this dreadful event and leave it buried deep inside my subconscious where I could never draw upon her image again. I would fail to remember the woman in the water, obscure any trace of memory altogether. Drown it all.

*Did she drown?* Was she awake when her body was torn apart? If only I could rewind and begin this day over, but I knew that was impossible and could never be undone and never be unseen. No, she was indelibly implanted behind my eyes and her bodily wreckage would replay again and again on my brain's projection screen. What kind of person could do such a hideous thing to another human being? Stomach acid bubbled up my throat. I began to feel woozy and sat down on the edge of the bed, sobbing into shaky hands. Tears seeped between my fingers.

*Get it together Molly,* I sniffed, then stood bracing for reality and went into the bathroom to splash cold water on my face. I checked myself in the mirror. My skin was pale and my swollen eyes resembled two piss holes in the snow. I wasn't surprised that crying would change my appearance. Everything about me, Hank, and the island had changed. No longer was it the idyllic little naïve village. We were no longer innocent.

Downstairs, coffee was brewing in the pot. The thick aroma made its way up the steps and into the bedroom. Hank must have put some on the stove. Yes, a hot liquid in my gut would do me some good right now. So would a large tumbler of bourbon. I took a deep breath, began dressing, and did my best at pulling myself together enough to join my husband downstairs.

Before I could do that, another bang came on the front door. "I'll get it," Hank shouted from the kitchen. I glanced down the stairwell, just able to see a bit at the right angle. Pushing the dogs aside, he opened the door to let Walter in. Bam was so excited by the company, he jumped up and French kissed Walt on the mouth.

"Jeeze Hank, what's wrong with that dog?" Walter wiped his mouth with his uniform's sleeve, spitting out a few dog hairs.

"Sorry Walt, he's been like that since we got him from the pound. That's the one bad habit I can't seem to break him of, or tearing up the trash, peeing on the crab baskets, wrecking the bedsheets into a ball, severe flatulence or rolling in dead stuff," Hank grinned.

Normally it's my job to discipline the dog, but since it was only Walt at the door, I was okay with his behavior.

Bam Bam, otherwise known as *Get Down* or *Stop it*, is our first and last rescue dog, or in his case, more like a salvage dog. He had been returned three times to the pound by previous owners in his first year. It only took about an hour after I had adopted the variegated-colored cattle dog to figure out why nobody else would put up with him. In the past, he had eaten numerous semi digestible items like a still-frozen turkey breast that was left thawing on the counter, a box of greeting cards, a bottle of vitamin E gel caps, three peanut butter cups, a chocolate bar, including the candy wrappers, and of course, the Ziploc baggie. But that was five years ago. His behavior has somewhat improved since, and even though he still snores loudly and hogs the bed, we have grown to love him in spite of his ridiculousness.

I peered downstairs again while brushing out a knot in my hair. Walt was saying, "Well, just keep him off me. I don't particularly care for his kind of romantic advances. Hey, is that coffee I smell? Good, I'm just in time. Got any cake to go with it?" Walter headed for the kitchen and pulled up a seat at the table and started massaging his sore knees.

"I figured you could use a cup by now." Hank poured three cups of the steamy black brew and fixed them up with milk and sugar, extra sugar for Walt. "Negative on the cake but we have donuts." Hank set down a box of Dunkin Donuts and two mugs of coffee on the table. Walter quickly grabbed two chocolate glazed beauties.

"That will do. Thanks. Where is Molly anyway?"

"Getting changed, she'll be down in a minute." Hank sipped his coffee. The morning events had begun to wear on him and he desperately needed the caffeine jolt.

"How's she doing? She didn't have much to say at the wharf."

"Fine, I guess. It's just a lot to take in for all."

As I came down the steps, their conversation pricked my ears. Hank's voice had taken on a serious tone and I needed to know what they were talking about but knew they would stop speaking the moment I came near. That made me hang back. If Walt turned, looked up, and saw me, I'd just come all the way down.

I know eavesdropping is ill-mannered and juvenile but that would never get in my way of pressing my ear to the wall.

"Do you have any idea what happened to that woman?" Hank cautiously inquired. The answer would be obvious and he didn't sound sure if he was ready to hear it.

"Doubt it was a boating accident. The body was severed pretty clean, which makes me fairly certain she wasn't torn up from a prop. No, somebody did that to her, no doubt."

"So, where is she now? Without I.D. you have no way of contacting her loved ones."

"Under the circumstances she'll remain at the medical examiners for a while until they do the initial autopsy. Her preliminary investigation revealed some significant bruising on her back and also a partial tattoo that appeared to be recently applied to the skin—the color hadn't faded into the darkish green ink shades yet. The bruising could have been caused post-mortem. That still needs to be determined, but the color of her skin when you found her indicates she could have been dead somewhere between three to five days. Of course, that would be under normal situations. Saltwater will cause premature bloating. That needs to be factored in as well. Her decomposition is what dictates the timeline. At eight to ten days after death, the body turns from green to red as the blood decomposes and the organs in the abdomen accumulate gas, but that's obviously not her case. And honestly, without the rest of her intact, it's near impossible to have an accurate account. Who knows how much of her the crabs had a go at?" Walter recited the facts while eating his donut without skipping a beat.

"How do you know about all this dead body stuff?" Hank was surprised by his friend's candor. Besides his sore knees from his years in the workforce, Walter is known by all as kind, caring and gentle in his ways to everyone, except towards me. Before his current stint with the department, Walter had put twenty-five years in with the Natural Resource Police, joining the force the day he graduated high school. The last thing he ever wants to do is haul a person off to jail. For the most part, his Sheriff's Department duties occupy his time by serving eviction notices, although he has been known to let the process drag on way past the due date, especially during colder winter months when he will personally escort evictees to a local shelter. But his favorite aspect of his job is driving his well-known Sheriff's Department cruiser with its highly visible gold star through Smithtown putting every waterman on high alert, just so he can hang his minnow bucket off the back of Hank's boat.

It's common for the NRP police to do a surprise spot inspection hoping to bag a waterman over his catch limit on the boat. He met Hank one hot summer afternoon on the water when he was pulling crab pots. Walter took his time making sure Hank was up to code. He checked for a current license, fire extinguisher, whistle, life jackets, and updated boat sticker. When he was through, Walter sat on the gunnel and they talked for a long while, mostly about fishing, and have been great friends ever since. I don't like it one bit because Hank has more fun with him than he does with me.

"Just some tricks of the trade I guess you learn from being on the job so long. Is there anymore coffee? "Walter asked.

"Sure, Walt. "Hank got up and poured the steamy brew into his cup with milk and extra sugar. "What did you mean by a partial tattoo? I don't remember seeing that on her skin."

"Think about it Hank, the other half of the tattoo was hacked off.

"That's a little gruesome don't ya think?"

"The crime committed on this woman is downright nothing but violent and gruesome. Chopping up a body and tossing it in the drink can only be done by something evil, some disturbing sick SOB. And let me tell you there are more of them out there than you can imagine, and I've seen plenty. Shoot, it's made so easy for them now."

"What do you mean, easier to do what?"

"It's easier for any malevolent mind out there lurking around, luring in their next victims. The super information highway does not discriminate against the sickos. There was a time when they hid underground on the dark web. Now it's all out in the open and they've repurposed the internet for their heinous acts in broad daylight, documenting their malicious plans in chat rooms and live broadcasts. Take a look at Facebook, for instance. Hordes of people watched when that nut bag announced his plan for a mass murder shooting and nobody tried to stop him, instead tuned in to see if he would actually do it. The people saw it unfold as he filmed the horror as if it was just another reality TV show. So who is the warped one now, the killer, or the ones enjoying the show?" Walter finished his second donut, contemplating a third.

"Yes, I remember hearing about that. "Hank shifted uncomfortably in his seat. "I don't like Facebook much, too many people ranting about this one and that one and the political tirades drives me up a wall. Ends a lot of friendships. And the thing about it is, the media wants its rating at any cost, eats it up for breakfast no matter who it destroys."

"I tell you, something awful is out there and rising in strength every day tugging at each and every one of our souls. Our society has become immune, complacent to violence, and worse, its enabler. We live our life through media. It's become accepting of disturbing movie images nightly on prime time TV. It's produced a culture of apathetic, navel-picking, attention-seeking, hyperrealism junkies. Deranged deviants are more empowered than ever by the internet and chances are, most people have innocently come across one or more deviant online. It's become acceptable for every type of abnormal fetish behavior to exist. The World Wide Web enables anyone looking for a partner to meet their disturbing habits, including cannibalism. I kid you not. Victims willingly run to their own demise. All the predators are let loose running Willy Nilly, the worst being sex crimes against children. Oh, sure the authorities have systems in place to safeguard neighborhoods since Megan's law was instituted. But it's not enough. Too many slip through the cracks. Law does not protect children from undetected predators. That's why the sex offender registry has only had a small impact on slowing down incidents."

"Yes, I remember when that went into effect." The mention of Megan's law made Hank stare down at his shoes and led me to do the same. Most people alive are aware of that highly profiled case responsible for the Sex Offender Registry, but no one was more aware of the little seven-year-old's rape and murder than me because it happened in my neighborhood, the very same neighborhood where I rode my bike and played kickball in the streets. The man responsible for her death had two previous convictions of sex crimes against small children, but nobody knew that when he moved in across the street from Megan and only a few blocks from my home. After her murder, Megan's parents went on a campaign to change the law to a mandatory community notification of sex offenders and Megan's Law was put into action. Her death bestowed fear in every parent's heart that nothing in our neighborhood or any other was ever going to be the same. It wasn't safe anywhere and no one was immune to its truth.

"It's an invisible war we are all engaged in and if you're not a spiritual man—and Hank I believe you are— but if you're not, then you better start working on it today because it's coming down on us all."

"I see what you mean, Walt. It's become a regular Sodom and Gomorrah revisited, hasn't it?" Hank answered. The words spoken by his friend were alarming, but even more frightening was that they were facts.

"Yeah," Walt sighed, "but I'm not so sure God is coming back this time and strike it down to the ground just to save mankind. I get the sense God isn't fond of do-overs."

"A long time ago I remember reading about something written by a Lakota prophet. Black Elk, I believe was his name. He said when the spider weaves his web around the world, it is near the end. Maybe he foresaw the internet and the damage it would cause to mankind."

"Look," said Walt, worrying about what he started. "You shouldn't pay so much attention to what I say. I promise this will all eventually work out. The authorities at hand will do everything possible to find who did this; it's just a matter of time. Nobody is resting until they do. When the local coroner gets done with their initial examination, she'll be sent to a forensic lab up in Salisbury for every intensive testing imaginable. I'm sure it's deemed a homicide by now. Tissue typing plus plenty of other tests will be performed on her. Probably by now, a team is searching data banks for similarities among women's homicides or for anything that could link the crimes. Trust me, this investigation will continue by the state police, on and off the water. Every marine authority available for miles around are out there now dragging metal grappling hooks across the sound. It's a good chance they'll find the rest of her somewhere under the water. The only thing I know for sure is it will be a while before anything substantial turns up. Hard to find a lead without the fingers for prints, but still, I'm confident they will come up with something to go on. The dismembering lacerations should reveal the cause of death."

"Cause of death? That's crazy Walt. It's obvious what killed her!" As though strangely heavy from this discussion, Hank stood from the table and hunched his shoulders over the kitchen sink.

"I know, I know but it still needs to be officially documented."

"But what about the tattoo, what are they doing about that?" I asked, magically appearing out from behind them.

Walt looked up. "How ya feeling Molly, are you doing okay? You must be shaken by what happened out there."

I shrugged a response. I wasn't really sure how I felt other than a little leftover shock from spending my morning with a partial dead body. It was obvious Walt was trying his best impersonation of being genuinely concerned about my wellbeing but I wasn't buying any of it. I knew his goal was to run me off track.

"Aw, you will be alright in time. You're a tough old broad," he patted my arm, which pushed my button to hot.

"And you're still fat," I snapped, causing Walter to drop his third donut.

Hank interjected, "I don't understand you two. You just don't get it, do you? Someone was murdered, her life was taken. The world has fallen down around our ears, but some things will never change no matter what happens, I guess. I wish just once you would both try being civil, for my sake?"

Hank was right. This wasn't the time to pick on Walter. I was certain there would be plenty of opportunities to insult him in due course. "I am sorry if I sounded inappropriate in any way about your girth, Walter. Now tell me about the tattoo. What did it look like?"

"Go on Walt, you can't win this one," Hank shook his head, "Might as well tell her about the tattoo."

"There's not much to tell about other than it was plain, just black, no other visible colors. It was more like a symbol or maybe like a logo of some sort. "

"But the tattoo drawing, Walt, what did it look like? A plant, a car or someone's name?" It felt like I was pulling teeth with a set of rusty eyebrow tweezers.

"It was thick in design. A dark bird, like an eagle, kind of military but not really. It was more retro and stylized."

"I don't remember seeing a tattoo on her." Hank stared at the ceiling trying to visualize the scene. "No, I don't think I saw one."

"No, you wouldn't have. It was on her middle lower back. And let's face it, not to be crude or anything, but her breasts kept her floating upright, a human life preserver."

"Yes, you're spot on about that. This is crazy." Hank put his hand to his forehead, rubbing it hard. I didn't say a word. This was all too insane, too surreal even for me to fathom.

"I have a photo on my phone I could show you but I think you both have seen enough for one day. Don't you?" Walter asked and we responded with mouths open so he continued his account.

"Look, I know a guy who's slicker than a boiled onion up in Salisbury who just so happens to be top-notch when it comes to the tattoo business. He knows all the talents within spit shot of the Delmarva area. I already emailed the police photos to his shop. If it was tatted anywhere near here, he would know. It's the only thing we have to go on for now. If any more information or body parts surface, you will be the first to know about it." Walt took a deep breath, pulled his body up from the table, and flipped on his sheriff hat before grabbing the last donut from the plate. "I need to be getting back to the office," he said with a heavy heart and turned towards the door.

Stopped by an afterthought, and looking at me, he added, "I already told you more than I should have and I trust it will stay right here in this kitchen. You know how Smithtown can spread a rumor quicker than a California fire in August. What happened here today is about as horrible as it can get and will probably haunt you a long while before you can begin to get on with your life. Remember that you're not in any way responsible for her death or her justice. Not one bit. Stay away from the town's talk; it will only make the work harder. Let the authorities handle it, it's our job."

Walter's words bombarded my thoughts with such accuracy striking a chord deep inside, causing me to shudder. There was a time when I believed everything was all innocence and sunshine, digesting every one of the Hardy Boys mystery books cover-to-cover, especially the ads on the last couple of pages depicting the idyllic life of young males—one big heroic adventure. The advertisements varied from pocket knives and model cars to various enrollments for summer camps in lush green pine-tree-filled forests surrounding a tea-stained lake, roped off for swimming drills. The ads boasted of a better life that only boys could own, offering excitement around every bend. Boys were blessed with all sorts of advantages I would never come to know.

My parents could never afford summer camp, not even the girl's day camp provided by the local Catholic Church on the other side of town. Oh, and of course pocket knives were certainly out of the question. They were taboo until one spring evening when my father had lent me his small ivory pocket knife for whittling sticks we'd use later that evening to roast hot dogs over a backyard fire. I knew there was no going back after that. I pored through the Hardy Boys mysteries set with a great passion. With every fading page, I was part of the enigma where I could live in a world that was only obtainable by boys. In a world where every crime was solved and the bad guy was sent to jail. I believed it all to be true, even possible. To me, the Hardy Boys were saviors of the universe and righteous in their victories. In some ways, I suppose I still believed and wished that to be true and hoped that someday it would be me, that I would be the hero in the story. I think about that every time I touch my father's pocket knife.

Walter left the house and the two of us sat alone in the kitchen where the silence lay heavy between us until I finally spoke. "But we have to do something about this, don't we?"

"Leave it alone Molly. This is pretty serious." Hank got up and put the mismatched coffee mugs in the sink, rinsing out what was left of the cold brew. I could tell by his stiff demeanor that this wasn't the appropriate time for a verbal joust right now; he was tired and my head was beginning to throb.

I said, "Maybe we should get out of here. Take a drive and get something to eat." I knew food was not on the agenda but it was as good as an idea any for clearing our heads, if that was even possible.

Hank shut the sink water off, dried his hands, and then came up behind, wrapping his arms around my shoulders. "Yeah, let's get out of here." He kissed the top of my head then plucked the truck keys from the hook. I instinctively followed behind.

"I love you. Do you know that?" I squeezed his hand with a newfound appreciation for my husband.

Hank's mouth stretched into a wicked smile. "Yes, ain't I the lucky one?"

## - *Two* -

It was early Saturday morning. The sun was making its way across the horizon, boasting a twinkling of light from dew left behind from the cool evening night. It tickled across the tops of the Needle Rush marsh in a syncopated dance moved by an invisible breeze's rhythmic vibrations.

I was still tired and should have slept in longer but summer's blinding sunshine through the window never allows for that, although I have to admit I do enjoy the wakening morning beauty that cast the room in purple-orange shapes. The cool, fresh early air that seeped through the kitchen window washed over my face, renewing my faith and leaving me thankful for waking up on the upside of the dirt ground.

Downstairs, I sipped the hot coffee, basking in colored rays that flooded the room, marsh hens clucked in low tide ditches, work-boats humming over the saltwater, all of which signaled the start of the day. I was filled with a sense of peace in the moment and held it close. But the feeling left abruptly, stinging me in the chest. The Crisfield Times spread open on the kitchen table glaring with inky blackened words was a clear reminder of how quickly a life can change, extinguished instantly, and dampened like a candle's flame. My heart sunk as I read the newspaper's sobering article.

*The Somerset County Police Department reported a woman's dismembered body was found on the Tangier Sound.*

*Two people were traveling by boat along Mine Creek at about 10:50 a.m. Wednesday, May 26th when they discovered the body part floating in the water, according to a Maryland State Police report. After securing the body the boaters then called 911. The Maryland State Police, the Somerset County Sheriff's Office and the Coast Guard were all dispatched to the site. The victim, who has not yet been identified other than female, was declared dead at the scene. The preliminary investigation indicates foul play, according to the report. The body will be sent to the Medical Examiner's office to determine the cause of death. No further information will be released until her next of kin have been notified.*

*The state police investigation into the incident is currently ongoing.*

"This is so wrong." I closed the newspaper and tried to picture what she could have looked like. Light or dark hair, maybe she had red hair and freckles? But I didn't remember seeing freckles. "Don't go there," I said through a deep breath, and headed out back. There was nothing I could do. It was best to not think about her. I fought the tears that formed in my eyes. Taking several deep breaths, I walked over to see my husband. Hank had been awake for hours painting the newly built crab floats in the back yard. His strength always brings a much-needed calmness to my soul. In his arms, I'm not afraid of anything.

"Good morning, sleepy head." Hank's clothes were covered in white paint. He was wearing his favorite T-shirt. It depicted a mermaid sitting provocatively on a giant fishhook, emphasizing her curvy butt.

"Yep, it sure is. You need some help?" I asked, without commenting on his shirt. Fish don't have asses! Everyone knows that, so why then are mermaids continually depicted with alluring bottoms? It drives me batty. Of course, it doesn't take much to drive me over the edge and something as silly as the silk-screened mermaid design will certainly do the job. Same goes for the phrase *mom jeans*. What the heck is a mom jean anyway? Is this something I'm supposed to need or want? This is the sort of inane dialogues that often fill our evenings whether Hank wants to talk about it or not. Luckily for me, he's very patient, never complaining and always accepting of my folly. He is perfect, aging gracefully as the years pass, becoming more handsome by the day. Funny, I never expected I would like him so much. Lord knows I try to be good like him; unwavering, decent, holding steadfast to that moral compass, always steering towards that straight line.

Unfortunately, my line is a little crooked, more like wavy potato chips. I truly do not know why my husband puts up with me. All I can figure is my lady parts must be magical.

"No, I'm good. Why don't you take a walk, get away from the fumes," Hank said without looking up. I wasn't sure which particular fumes he was referring too. There were plenty of odors wafting across the yard from the rank crab house. The thick summer heat is hot enough to steam a crab that's left behind on the scorching gel-coated deck, poor things unable to escape from boiling to an orange hue by the sizzling hot sun. Odors linger across the boat's deck, creating a whole other gambit of smells as the sun bakes dry shad bunker bait, permanently fusing to the gunnels' fiberglass. At low tide, fermenting micro debris bubbles its stench upward from the black marsh mud. These are the now-familiar smells of Smithtown's summer crabbing season. They are about as comforting as achieving a worthy vomit after suffering from a sour stomach.

The truth about living on the water is the fetid smell of a dead crab is never forgotten. Crab season is also no stranger to the summer's longer daylight hours that coincide with longer work days, and just like all the other watermen, Hank is overworked, exhausted, and cranky. I sometimes call him Mr. Snappy Ass, out of earshot of course, which usually needn't be too far because of his damaged hearing from the boat's engine noise. I don't mind being upset by his testy moods now and then because he is far too handsome to keep up that nonsense.

I still have a juvenile crush on the man. The slightest scent of his skin takes away my air and any sense of reason. He is kryptonite to my super powers, breaking down all my defenses with one fell swoop.

In reality, it's the crab season that makes me angry. It's directly responsible for my loneliness on this island. I rarely see my husband this time of year. Hank, if he isn't working, he's asleep catching up on rest, making me miss him even when he is home. At least his winter job with the state Wildlife Management gets him back by five. Pulling out possums wedged in drain sewers or an owl from a chimney is finished before dark.

I hate the crab season. It is responsible for my becoming the bored, cranky, crabby wife. The years of experience has taught me to how to endure the solitude of the crab house days. The women of Smithtown are kept working behind the scenes for their husbands and their survival. They're wed and bedded to the crab house, left behind spending most of the day alone fishing up soft crabs from the floats. Cleaning pump pipes clogged with periwinkle snails, sea grass, or the occasional minnow, or *minnas*, as the locals call them, sucked up a pipe during high tide, is honest work and in theory should afford me great pride. There is something to be said about idle hands being the devil's work. I used to have a busy life as an artist, painting landscapes, but the market is not the same since the housing crash. At least I can keep myself occupied, which is always safer for all involved since I really should never ever be left to my own devices.

Often I have to remind myself that I voluntarily signed up for this tour and loneliness is commonplace and part of the fallout. I have learned to accept while I relish the warm sunny days when the fair weather weekenders return to the island.

I went back inside to fetch the dogs for a walk. Sara Jane was sound asleep on the cool tile floor. She is as sweet and lovely as her name. Black labs in general are adored by all but Sara was particularly blessed with a way of melting even the hardest of hearts at first glance, and she knows it. She's bred from a hardy hunting stock yet displays a delicate structure. She is cracking on in years, reaching past the age of fifteen, which I am told is long time for a larger dog. Her eyes are clouded with cataracts and the arthritis has taken over her body. A monthly hour-and-a-half car trip to the specialized veterinary care, where she receives a large dose of laser therapy, has kept her upright and able to walk. It's expensive, but she's worth every penny. It would make more financial sense to just get it over with and add her name to my rising credit card account.

I stood over the sleeping lab and spoke her name, but her body remained motionless. "Sara?" I started to panic, and quickly knelt down to touch her breathless side. "Sara? Sara Jane?" No response. I shouted her name again, shaking her shoulder. "Sara!"

Her head jerked upward in surprise, blinking through squinted eyelids. "Aw baby girl," I crooned, stroking her velvety soft ears. Bam rolled his jealous fat body off the couch and pawed my leg for equal attention.

"Walkies?" That was enough to excite a move towards the door. It was still an early sun. The humidity would be light, making the walk pleasant though we won't go too far because of Sara's arthritic legs. They have all but given way, and my only hope is that she passes painlessly in her sleep before I have to face the unthinkable, which I don't think I am brave enough to do.

"Come on lets go," I commanded, and we headed out into a pretty day. Sara Jane trotted about, sniffing every fox pee territorial marking as the fiddler crabs scurried across the road waving their over-sized claws in defense.

I have read many books about Maryland's eastern shores. Some were written by the great writers and some were written by not-so-famous locals, and have found they all were chock full of heroic adventures that romanticized life on the water. Truth be told, in reality it's a frightening and unforgiving terrain. The wind's constant hard blow can knock one off balance onto the ground. There are times when I cannot open my house's front door from the wind's terrific force. I've even seen it freeze waves in mid-air, and toss one onto another until it's frozen solid enough to walk all the way across the sound. I've felt the harshest of winds rage without warning, smash anything in its path, rip through siding, tearing roofs from houses, and thrust water and sea life onto the roads, leaving flopping fish behind while it recedes to its normal level.

Yes, I maybe I did come here voluntarily but I sure didn't know what I was getting into. I'm from New Jersey, the land of strip malls, air conditioning and pizza. And it's a well-known fact that Jersey girls glow in the dark and can take on anything and everybody. If that's true I must be considered the runt of the litter.

I'm not the only island inhabitant who has suffered from the wrath of weather. Residents have lived in peril since its beginning by early Anglo Saxon settlers. To this day, the islander's accent is a mix of European British for which time has morphed its sound into something of its own that has been rounded off by the sea. The idea that they choose to live in this forsaken environment constantly amazes me, especially back when life was generally more difficult to envision. How they ever scratched out a salt ridden existence in the relentless forces of nature is beyond me. At least I have access to running water, air conditioning, strip malls, and thank the Lord for small miracles like bug spray.

Not many can appreciate the beauty Smithtown has to offer. Though it is at times isolated and untouched, its rhythm runs naturally between weather elements, nature, and its inhabitants. They intertwine with each one becoming part of the other's fabric. When people ask me

about what I think about living here, I just smile and say
it's not for everyone. Now I barely remember my life back
before the hurricanes, water spouts and flood tides. That
was before I married Hank and moved to a tiny island in
the lower eastern shore of Maryland. That was long
before I joined the island life. I remember the day we
were joined together in matrimony down by the water in
Smithtown. It was pretty the whole month of September,
with most of the biting insects absent and the sun shining
its best. When the preacher asked for the "I do," after a
slight hesitation on my part, I actually said yes with one
hundred and forty of Hank's closest friends as witnesses
just in case I said "No." It was the first wedding in
Smithtown's history and I blame the historical event for
sinking the island three inches from the weight of the cars
and people that joined us that day.

Smithtown does have its brief moments of beauty in
all the seasons and at times it's breathtaking. Unlike other
places, such us western Pennsylvania with its watercolor
washes of gray-toned skies, the sunset's color is honest
and unfiltered and the sun will shine twelve months out
of the year in Smithtown.

My eyes followed a soaring osprey scouting a meal
from the water maintaining his mesmerizing flight high
above the *kleeklee* chirps from its mate who impatiently
waits on her nest of sticks. I can hear the Canadian
Geese's crackling voices bounce over the sound. It's hard
to pinpoint where they may be for the water can play

tricks on your ears and fool your eyes. At times, the oyster boats appear to magically float in the air. It can amplify the waterman's chatter, carrying voices for miles and I have learned to be careful of what I said outside, for in a small town with a population of nine people, gossiping was a sporting event.

I noticed the wind slowing, becoming nearly absent, turning the water into slick cam, highlighting the crab boats out past the point where the rough wind will part and release its cool soothing relief to the working boat's mates.

"Yes it's all so enchanting until a fly tears flesh from your bones," I swore under my breath, swatting a greenhead from my leg, blood dripping down to my ankle. Smithtown can certainly boast of its parade of seasonal biting insects, gnats, fairy mosquitoes, mayflies, deer and sheet flies. Out of all the pesky bugs, I detest greenheads the most. We continued our walk to the first bridge; here the comet's crater ridge is visible. Hard to believe that once upon a time these little strings of islands were created by falling comet strikes.

"Bam, wait," I called, startled by his howls as he set off chasing the Smithtown eagle like he really had a chance of catching the massive bird. There isn't another canine alive that can come close to his determination. That dog sure has hope.

"I see you got him trained real good, Molly," an amused voice rose behind me. I didn't have to turn around to know it was Earl Leigh watching from inside the crab shack with its red and pastel green paint peeling on the tin shack's sides. His crab floats are shut down now; most are falling apart from the weeded intrusion. A metal burn barrel sits disintegrating by the side of the road. Without the coming and going of his 1960's rusting red classic truck, the property would appear left abandoned with little evidence of how life used to be when crab houses were running full tilt all hours of the night. Other than the tenderly planted zinnia flower beds, to anyone else passing by, they would only assume it vacant.

An abrasive melody floated from inside the shack that pulled both the dogs curiously to the door. *"Never marry a banjo player — tell you the reason why — he's got tobacco stuck in his teeth and he never zips his fly."* It was still early in the morning but I could tell Earl was well into his daily constitution of vodka. A plague that only seems to affect watermen severely since the work day starts in the early dark morning, only to end too early in the day with nothing else to do but indulge that thirst.

I always considered Earl Leigh resembling a bit of a cartoon with wiry hair jetting out from under a greasy ball cap and suspenders that held up his broken zippered pants. Often, when he stops by the house for a visit, Hank prefers I stay in the house while they talk with Earl Leigh's rusty truck parked in our driveway for the better part of an hour as he tells stories through his animated locally accented voice while polishing off his bottle du jour. He's worn inside and out. His body has surrendered to a permanent stiffness from years of hard times culling out his life of crabbing on the water. Most people won't bother with him but I stop to chat when he's outside when I am passing. Earl Leigh has more knowledge filed in his brain than all the watermen put together. It's a given that he will always compliment a pretty woman or anything female, I suspect. I truly enjoy his stories if they bare any truth or not. "What's the point of being a good liar if everyone believes you?" he would say.

Although I never met her, he would tell me that I remind him of his old flame which would cause him to go soft and teary-eyed when speaking of his forgotten love. There is a kind lilt in his voice that erupts with tenderness from somewhere deep inside when he tells of his sweetheart. Over the years, they'd had at best, a coarse relationship, much to the town's entertainment. Rumor has it that late one night she doused his crab floats with motor oil because she had caught him flirting with the post office lady. The oil deprived the crabs of oxygen, killing every critter in the floats. After finding the crab carnage in the morning, he became so fired up with anger that he sought revenge by spraying her prize rose bushes with weed removal chemicals, destroying every leaf and bud. Their spiteful actions ruined any hope of a reunion after that.

"Come on in, bring them hounds with ya," he gestured towards the door, "I'll make us some tea." My gut had insisted on staying put, but instead of heeding its wisdom, I entered the shack. The place was surprisingly neat with a cooling breeze from the one scrubby tree shading the shack's roof. The rickety building was nestled by water-filled guts. Hank would kill me if he knew I was in here alone but I figured it was safe enough with Bam by my side. Besides, Earl Leigh would be too high to even remember to divulge our visit to anyone.

"How ya doing? "I asked.

"Still dying on schedule I suppose," he laughed.

"I like the song you were playing, did you write that one?"

"Nah I don't have no talent like that. You can sit down here for your tea," But instead of tea, Earl poured vodka into two smudged glasses, then set one in front of me.

"Thank you." I politely lifted the glass to my lips. *He can't be expecting me to drink this straight up?* I glanced around at the shack and noticed what must be his bedroom and the bottom of the door that was cut several inches short. "Can I ask what happened to the bottom of your door?"

"Ha, I altered the length so it wouldn't hurt my toes as much when she slammed the door in my face," he laughed and then downed the vodka in one swallow, exhaling the heavy aroma.

The dogs snooped around the perimeter with Sara investigating every item. I kept a tight watch on Bam, who was eyeing up the half-dead potted plant that sported a sun-faded yellow bow, just in case he decided to relieve himself on the stem. I couldn't help but wonder who would have cared enough to have given Earl Leigh a plant. "That might need watering," I pointed towards the pot, but knew the shanty never had running drinking water, leaving the plants' survival low on the totem pole. The only water that runs into his shack is salted, and by looking at the condition of his squirrely hair, I suspect he may be using it for bathing. Around the back of the shanty is a fully operating outhouse privy next to the crick, which if it were known by the Maryland Department of Environment would probably set them into a full-blown fit. Earl Leigh was content with his living situation and has been an outskirts Smithtown resident much longer than I ever will be and pretty much knew everyone there is to know around here. I wanted to pump him for info on anything he might know about the murder, but decided to ease into the conversation.

"Sure has been a lot of high water in the roads lately. Do you give any stock to this Global Warming hoopla and rising tides? They say all the shorelines will be underwater soon."

"Don't worry your pretty little head about it. We never finished the first ice age. You will be dead by then anyway so no need to get all angst about it. It's just these blasted east winds blowing water up the creeks. The politicians are only in it for themselves—pay no mind to their scare tactics."

"I hope you're right." I was in no position to argue with him since he most likely knew more about global warming than me; actually, my dogs probably know more about it than I do.

"I know I'm right. Water level has been the same for years, too high or too low to get any crabbing done." He stopped talking, leaned back and looked dead on at me. "So what's really on your mind, young lady? I can tell something is stuck in your craw. You don't want to talk about high water do you?"

"No, I suppose not."

"You wanna talk about what happened out there," he pointed out to the sound.

"Yes, I do. I think you can help me."

"Some bad stuff went down in Smithtown. We've never been touched by evil like this before and it's changed all of us for good. We were wrong to think we were different, safe and secure from evil. It seeps through the smallest fissure. Its patience is endless and it will wait for its opportunity, for that one perfect particle of time, the moment when God looks away."

My stress level heightened with each word he voiced in that serious tone. He was frightening and profoundly spot-on but not enough for me to cease questioning. "That person who was released from jail recently, do you think he could have anything to do with it? I heard he came back to Fairview, to his old place. Is it true the guy would beat women and extinguish cigarette butts on their bodies? I heard that the police found it difficult to charge him with anything but a minor drug offense because he would threaten those women if they ratted him out?"

"Whoa, slow down there and take a breath. If you mean that weasel Nate, yeah, heard he was out of the pokey as well. Hell, he ain't that smart enough to pull off a something like that, though he can be slicker than a pocket full of chocolate pudding, he just ain't got all his circuits firing."

From time to time I have been guilty of repeating idle chatter but really I hate it when someone starts their sentence with the words *I heard*, because usually nine times out of ten it's only malicious gossip designed to inflict unfounded damage on the unknowing person and ultimately it sucks me right in the middle each time. However, the town's talk was fairly consistent that Nate had been stealing gas from the workboats to fill his truck's tank. Crab pots started to disappear, lawnmowers and power tools, too. Turns out he was selling to an auction house on the other side of the bay. People were more than fed up with their belongings going missing in the middle of the night. Sometimes, he even operated during the daylight hours when kids were at school and the parents were off to work, leaving the empty houses easy pickings.

"See what's happened here, Molly, is your mind is all caught up in a mess that ain't yours and it's brought you to an impasse."

"A what?"

"An impasse is a fork in the road of life."

"Oh."

"You do know what to do when you come to a fork in the road do ya, Molly?"

"I suppose so," I sighed, waiting for the old joke.

"Well, when you come to a fork in the road, all you can do is take it." Earl Leigh laughed so hard it jarred his upper dentures loose to slide around in his mouth. "Uh oh. I was pulling up a crab pot this morning when my teeth fell in the crick, had to use a net to fish the buggers up from the mud bottom. They never did fit me right since I got em last year. That's what you get with that damn government insurance." Embarrassment washed over his face and he turned his head away, adjusting his dentures. "Aw, the hell with them," he grumbled, and shoved the upper denture deep in his pocket, smacking his lips. "That's better." Earl Leigh poured a small shot of vodka into a smudged glass, then handed it to me, motioning to chug it down, which I did.

"Thanks," I said. The words burned in my mouth.

"You know, I remember a time when that fella was something to see. Had a lot of money from his daddy, spent it on big man toys like helicopters and fancy speed boats. He was good looking to boot with an innocent face, which is how he gets away with it all. The partying started night after night. But after a while, none of these things gave him thrills anymore except for that little white lady addiction he had. That's where all the money went — right up his hooter, lost everything to it. Now he bums cigarettes, pocket change and beer. He'll steal everything, including the shoes on your feet while you're sleeping. Plumb pitiful really, he could have turned out better, gone a different route instead of stealing gas and crabs from work-boats. Nobody believed he was thieving because he had one of them likable faces. Now we lock up everything tight at night. Times are not what they use to be in Smithtown or anywhere else for that matter. I know what I'm talking about; I've been on God's green earth longer than I deserve." His voice trailed off, as he took another swig, staring at the remaining Vodka sloshing in the bottle.

"A while back, Victor Handy hung out with Nate. He was a skinny dark-skinned guy, could have been African American but not sure. See 'em both at the pool hall. Thick as thieves they were until one day Nate turned up alone and was from then on. Nobody knew what happened to Victor until he turned up face down in a ditch."

"A ditch?" I asked.

"Yep, deader than a doornail."

"Dead from what?"

"High tide I guess. One of them mosquito breeding tidal ditches." Earl Leigh gave the bottle another swirl and swallowed another shot. A glistening came over his eyes. He was getting hammered and that was my clue to leave.

"Thanks, Earl Leigh for your hospitality. Guess I should be going now." I walked towards the door with dogs close behind.

"Any time darling, any time." Earl Leigh winked then rolled back into his chair for what I believed to be a very long nap.

I should not have been surprised when Walter drove down the road just in time and to see me leave the shanty. That's how my luck rolls. I paid him no mind as he slowed the cruiser down to a crawl then slid the window down.

"You do know gossip 'round here travels faster than a cold sore in January."

"Then keep your pie hole shut," I snapped. "What are you doing snooping around Smithtown anyway? Aren't you out of your district? Shouldn't you be busy rescuing kittens from the treetops?"

"Hank asked me to check up on you, good thing too. By the looks of it, I'm just in time." Walter sniffed the air, "Have you been drinking?"

"Stop making a big deal out of this, we were just talking." Suddenly banjo music rippled through Earl Leigh's window accompanied by slurred drunken verses.

Walter swung his head towards the shanty, then shot me a look. I moved to block his line of vision, muffling the sound.

"Talking? I seriously doubt it. I would bet my last donut that you were pumping him for info, enjoying an early happy hour." Walter worriedly glanced over at the near-empty Dunkin Donut box riding shotgun on the seat.

"Wow, that sounded like a serious and intentional wager. Don't worry; I know for my safety it's best to never get between you and food, not even one tiny crumb." The effects of the vodka were lingering, but still, I was confident I could take him on.

"I'll tell Hank you're fine then."

"He knows I am. He's at the house."

"Well if he's working, I won't bother him." Walter turned the squad car around then shouted out the window before speeding away. "You're welcome!"

I flipped him the bird and continued walking home, hoping to make it there before he called Hank, but like I said before, my luck don't roll that way.

## - *Three* -

Hank was in the yard when I arrived at the house. He was preoccupied assembling new crab pots with buoys, ropes and plastic orange rings as well as something I didn't recognize.

"What's with the metal rectangles?" I asked before he could mention Walter's phone call.

"Turtle excluders, they're called. New Maryland regulations require them on every pot."

"What do you mean excluder?"

"They get their head stuck in the funnel; it keeps the turtles from drowning." Hank piled the crab pot on top of the others stacked in the bed of his white pickup truck. I never understood why all the watermen drive white pickup trucks. I wondered if that was a Maryland regulation as well.

"I'm dropping the new pots in the water after I finish working on the gear. Want to go with me?"

"Sure. How long before we leave?" I really needed a snack of some sort to soak up the vodka.

"About an hour. Be ready to go, okay? You can run the boat for me." Hank walked closer and kissed me. I think he just wanted to check my breath for alcohol. "Little early for cocktails don't ya think?"

"I don't want to talk about it." I knew Walter had called him. I believe it's how Walt receives the most enjoyment in life, by making me squirm. I hurried back in the house and had enough time to change, cover my practically transparent fair skin with sunscreen, and check my email. I sat down at the desk with a box of *Nabisco Cheez-Its*, flicked on the laptop, and munched on a highly nutritious breakfast of golden crackers while checking my email. As usual, there was nothing interesting or of great importance. Still, I kept up with it anyway as if one day it would change my life for the better.

I closed the tab and opened up a Facebook window to see the usual pictures of people's pets and grandchildren I do not know. I checked my notifications next, only to see pictures of people's lunches. Maybe it's me, but I don't get it. I have no idea what the fascination about publicly documenting your meal is about.

I still had time to kill. I could do the dishes or laundry but tooled around on the internet instead. I looked at the clothing sales happening at the mall, which was absurd because I never go there. I barely shop for anything to begin with, let alone clothes, and I never step foot in a mall. Amazingly, I can find my way home blindfolded from the middle of a dark forest but leave me alone in a mall and I'll have to dial 911 for help. It's not my fault, shopping malls lack natural light. I can't help it if I get lost.

I wasted another ten minutes reading the news. After finding nothing new, I typed: *Missing tattooed women in the Delmarva area* in the search bar. I was shocked at the search engine's response.

*Woman drowned after husband closed lid on the hot tub. Police arrested Timothy Johnson after drowning his wife during a domestic altercation. The report states that Johnson slammed the lid closed but did not mean to kill his wife, just shut her up. Johnson is currently awaiting trial.*

"Maybe he should have tried marriage counseling instead, big dope," I mumbled, and scrolled through the next article that caught my eye from the San Francisco Times.

*Police in San Francisco are investigating after a headless body was found in a fish tank earlier this month. The body was found at the home on Clara Street near 5th in the SOMA neighborhood. Officers investigated complaints of suspicious odors inside the residence and after receiving a search warrant found a body in a large fish tank inside a room near the stairway. The body was without a head or hands.*

Similar murders but no cigar. An east and west coast murder couldn't be connected, though. I wondered if I should call Walter and tell him what I found. "Leave me alone and stop this insanity Molly," is all he would say. I continued to read the next article.

*New photos released of sisters found duct taped along Hudson River. Police have released new photos of the two women whose duct-taped bodies were found washed up along the Hudson River. WABC-TV reports, the bodies of 16-year-old Terry Fowler and 22-year-old Robin Fowler, of Fairfax, Virginia, were found around 2:30 p.m. Wednesday in the vicinity of 68th Street and Riverside Park. Responding officers found the bodies lying on rocks near the river. The women were last seen on April 24. A police source told WABC that the bodies were bound together with duct tape around their waists and feet so that they were facing each other. Both were fully clothed, and there were no signs of trauma. Sources believe the bodies washed ashore with the tide and stayed when the tide went out. The Medical Examiner's Office will determine the cause of death, and the investigation is ongoing.*

My heart was pounding faster than I could read the follow-up article about the sisters. I was on to something big. Could this possibly tie the Smithtown murder to their case?

*In recent days, the NYPD sent detectives to Virginia to help unravel the lives of the two sisters. At first, police suspected they died in a suicide pact and said there was no evidence of a crime. But that thinking may now be changing, and sources say police now have a better sense of where the two entered the water and how long they may have been in the water.*

*The NYPD is also asking for the public's help in solving what happened to the women.*

Okay, maybe I was onto nothing. My cell phone rang and I almost peed myself.

"How ya doing kiddo? I heard about the tragic incident all the way up here in Baltimore." It was Julie, one of Smithtown's fair-weathered part-time residents and my dear friend. I missed her dearly and barely got to see her anymore. All of my friend's lives had evolved and moved on without me.

"Are you and Hank okay?"

I was not surprised the news had already traveled to the big city. It was pretty tragic, and that kind of news generates money.

"It was on the local Baltimore news station. Boy, that story has more twists than a pretzel factory."

"I know, it sounds scary but we really are fine." I didn't let on it was worse than she could imagine. "No need in worrying about us." I tried making light of her rising stress level, although her concerns about what I might get into were warranted. I once went chasing an insane idea about the location of a missing duck hunter during a hurricane out on Piney Island, and in a kayak to boot. The weather roared up ugly and I took shelter in an abandoned shack. But I fell through the rotted floorboards, landing next to the dead duck hunter. Hank and Walter had found me bloody and barely breathing. I was stupid but happy to be alive. I wasn't ready to meet my maker and I don't think He was ready to meet me either.

"Good to know you both are well. Is there something I can do for you?" Julie asked.

"If only you could," I sighed. Long-distance friends or not, I was fortunate to have so many kind and generous people in my life and Julie reigns on the top of that list. "Can I ask you something?"

"Sure Molly, anything." She said after a slight hesitation. "Ask away."

"Have you ever heard that dead bodies can sit up?"

"I can't say that I have."

"I heard they can. If the body builds up enough gas, that can cause it to moan or change positions."

"Sounds like a party to me," Julie snickered.

"I also read that most people will die in their beds, but the majority of the remaining will die sitting on the commode. Isn't that an attractive ending?"

"Molly Hanson, you're bored and searching that infernal internet again, and conjuring up all sorts of ideas, aren't you? And I bet you're involved deeper in that woman's death." Sheila knew me all too well.

"I'm trying my best not to, but we both know that refraining is not in my nature."

"Does Hank know what you're up too?"

"He might, but I doubt it. Besides, I'm not doing anything wrong."

"Not yet! Promise me you'll be careful?" Julie's tone had changed. Stressing out my friend was not my agenda, but I had a tendency to stretch my friendships to a breaking point.

"I will, don't worry."

"I read a little phrase by Confucius and it instantly reminded me of you."

"Never spit upwind?"

"Nope."

"Tell me then."

"Life is really simple, still we insist on making it complicated."

"I see your point." My friend Julie can be way smarter than Confucius.

"I'll tell you something else I learned recently," I said.

"Go on."

"Did you know that every year a large number of people die on special occasions?"

"What do you mean by special occasion? Like, what, are you saying that the moment I read the words *Buy one get one free* I'll keel over on the spot?"

"No, silly." My friend's laughter is far superior to any medicinal cure invented. "Holidays are stressful. There's a surge in heart attacks during Christmas."

"Gee wiz, that's a cheery thought. I will keep that in mind next year."

"Of course if you think about it, there is one thing for certain about death," said Julie.

"What's that?"

"If you wait around for it long enough, it will come."

"I swear you are a mess and the only one who can make me laugh about death. I better ring off now. Hank is probably waiting for me. Good to hear your voice again."

"Watch your back, Molly. Take care of yourself." Julie sniffled.

"I will," I said and pressed the end button on the keypad. She was right. I should stay out of this. I was beginning to spook myself. But that wouldn't happen, and I reluctantly shut the computer down.

Hank poked his head through the back door and yelled across the kitchen, "You ready yet?"

"Yes, be right there." Quickly I threw several water bottles in a plastic Walmart shopping bag, tossed two cookie treats to the dogs, and headed out the door, slamming it closed behind me.

We packed the boat with new crab pots, stacking them high on one another until it blocked my vision. Hank stood up on the bow, navigating the way by pointing straight, left, and right. I've done this many times before but running the boat without being able to see the water is unnerving. He really shouldn't have as much confidence as he does in my ability to handle this; I sure don't.

"See the plum tree on the island?" Hank asked.

"No, not really. I can't see a thing but wire."

"How about now? Is that better?" Hank moved several of the crab pots out of my line of sight.

"Yes, I can see it."

"Good, keep the boat heading straight for the tree." Hank heaved the pots overboard, spacing them evenly apart. I never liked working on the water but sometimes I help him because it offers me time with my husband. I love watching his taunt, tanned body and his muscular arms whirling the crab pots over his head as if they were light as cotton balls.

Hank threw the last pot, then inhaled deeply. "Last one, thank goodness." He twisted the plastic lid from a water bottle, downed the contents in seconds, and then glanced back at me. "You held the boat on course for six strings of crab pots. You did well." He smiled for a change. "Why don't you run the boat ashore on Oyster Island for a while? Take a break."

"I would love that."

"Maybe make out behind a water bush." Hank always knows what to say to ease my mind. He knew it was my favorite secret place. I liked to call it Oyster Island although that's not its real name. It's lined with several freshwater ponds, a long beach to explore, and a cool endless breeze that keeps the greenheads at bay. Often we bring the dogs to splash the water as we snorkel for treasures, finding old bits of pottery and medicine bottles that remained behind from another time period.

We were not very far away from my favorite island and landed in no time at all. Hank threw out the anchor then pulled on the line, wedging it in the sandy bottom. I hopped out of the boat, landing in the saltwater. Minnows frantically scattered away as I tromped, splashing through the clear water.

On Oyster Island, I am a child again, released from reality's weight. I turned my face towards the sun with arms stretched upward absorbing its goodness. Further down the sandy beach, angry oystercatchers squawked as I walked too close to their nest, flashing oversized deep orange beaks in warning. On the other side where the waves crash, the island's side cutting away the landscape is the area for finding treasures; vintage sea glass from old spice bottles, bits of animal-shaped driftwood, and unusual shells. It became more beautiful with each turn over a sand dune. Careful not to cut my feet as I passed through the sea drift, I continued the length of the island to where I could walk no further without sinking into the black mud. Looking over my shoulder, I couldn't see Hank. Out here there are no clocks, schedules or televisions. Without these daily measurements of time, it's easy to lose bearings. The thought reminded of my parents saying, "Guess you don't have to keep time anymore."

I stood still for a moment and let the wind blow my hair recklessly even though it would take hours to untangle. I wondered why Hank didn't follow me, and decided to go back to where he sprawled out on the sand fast asleep. Lying down next to him, I touched his hand, listening to the wave's lullaby until it coaxed me to sleep.

The sun had changed position by the time I awoke from the sophomoric sounds of laughing gulls circling the sky for their last meal of the day. It was later than I thought. Hank was standing by the water, checking the tide.

"How long was I asleep?"

"Long enough for your skin to turn red. We better get a move on. Tide's going out fast."

I gave a little yawn and shook the sand from my hair, then hopped in the boat. Hank pulled the anchor in, started up the motor, and steered the boat for home. "Did you enjoy the day?" he asked.

"Very much, thank you. It's so beautiful here."

"Thought we needed some alone time. I miss you." Hank pulled me close and kissed me hard like he used too, sending goosebumps all the way down to my hoo-ha. I was floored. This was not the cranky crab man I knew then. This was the handsome husband I remember, and I kissed him back, holding on tight all the way home.

After tying up the boat, Hank went straight to the crab house and set off immediately in cleaning several trays of soft crabs. My stomach's growls had signaled it was time to figure out what the heck I was going to be fixing for dinner tonight. Should be easy enough; Hank likes anything smothered in gravy. Don't make a difference to him, be it homemade, packaged, or canned. He can't stand eating a pea, but he would eat a whole bowl full if it was covered with gravy. Gravy pot roast, gravy fries, gravy noodles with gravy, and fried mash potato soup. I swear he would be completely content if I poured gravy over his morning cereal.

Who am I to talk? I can't comment on his appetite's preference since my favorite food hands-down would have to be a cheese and ketchup sandwich on white bread.

"We better go out to the crab house see what his gravy heart desires," I said to the dogs and let them out the door. They ran off into the yard, sniffing the grass. Hank didn't look up when I walked into the crab house. His mood had quickly morphed back into his work mode.

"You should be getting hungry by now. What would you like for dinner?"

"I don't care, just whip up something."

"Okay, I'll figure it out," I replied, leaving the crab house, but before I could reach the back door I heard Hank holler out across the yard.

"With gravy please."

## - *Four* -

It was his first inspection since graduating six months ago from the Department of Natural Resource Police academy training camp. Anticipation held the blonde twenty-six-year-old officer straight as a ruler in the bucket seat of the black truck with inscribed gold lettering that boldly announced his presence. A slight rain fell on the windshield, complicating visibility, as his eyes darted between the slapping wipers probing the wide expanse of water for a sign of one particular workboat's return. Searching for his target through his department-issued binoculars, he thought he had seen movement and adjusted the lens to read the name of the first boat returning, *The Shelly Lynn*.

"All systems are a go. Request instructions." Remaining calm, the officer spoke into the two-way radio.

"Proceed as planned. ETA backup two minutes," the truck's receiver clicked a scratchy response. The officer knew he had to be on his game, maneuvering quickly to their wharf before being spotted. Timing was everything. The element of surprise would hinder any chance of the illegal undersized crabs from being pitched overboard before his inspection. The officer put the truck in reverse, turning it around towards the private boat docks and headed down the narrow lane which was blocked by a maroon van parked sideways in the road. With his hot pursuit brought to a standstill, the officer wailed on the horn signaling with his hands to clear the vehicle from the road.

"Out of the way, move it!" he shouted in frustration, but the driver of the van didn't budge. Aggravated, the officer blew the horn again until the van slowly pulled alongside the department's black truck. The window slid down letting out a huge puff of cigarette smoke dissolving under raindrops.

"I'm here to tell you something important and you better listen to every word I'm telling ya. You're gonna have a dead body on your hands if that idiot Nate Herford even steps his big toe on my property. I'm gonna blast it off with my shotgun then shoot what's left of his sorry ass. And you can mark my words in your little shiny notebook." It was Ole Man Keller, who rarely left his home. Stays to himself mostly and doesn't say much either unless he's provoked to anger. And right now he was madder than a hornets' nest jostled by a ten-year-old boy's rock. Local lure says it takes a good bit to rile him up, but when it happens, it's always best to give him a wide birth.

"Mr. Keller, calm down now and tell me what is going on from the start." Before he began this assignment, the young officer had an office briefing about the natures of Rumbley Harbor's colorful residents. He was well aware of Ole Man Keller's reputation.

"Okay if you want to play grown-up cop, sure then, I'll tell ya what that dumbass did. I was sitting there on my porch having a can of beer and a cigarette, just minding my own business on my own property. Far as I know, a man still has that right, unless them city liberals took that away too!"

"No sir, you still have that right." The officer knew it was an offense to threaten bodily harm, but he also knew everything he'd heard about Ole Man Keller was true and getting hotter by the minute. "Maybe you can just tell me what happened without shooting anyone."

"Like I said, I was just sitting there thinking about what to do with a big pile of dirt in the bucket of my front end loader when this jackass pulled into my driveway asking for a cigarette and I said that I didn't have any more. Then he asked for a beer and I told him no to that as well and he turned around and walked right into my house and helped himself to one of my beers. You never mess with a man's beer, let alone go in his house without being invited in, right?"

"No, sir," the officer sighed.

"He's not right in the head I tell ya. I didn't want no trouble so I suggested to get moving along, which he did right on over to the house next to me. He started banging on their door and windows but no one answered him. I think they were hiding in there. Anyway, it started to rain so I went to put my loader back in that garage, when here comes this idiot waltzing back across my property and went right back inside my house and got himself another beer. Can you believe it? I couldn't get off my loader fast enough. I wanted to crack his skull open at that point but he took off before I could get a hold of him. But if I had, he'd find his body donated to science before he was done using it and they'd be arresting my ass instead of his."

"Mr. Keller, I'm afraid I cannot do anything for you. It's not our department's area, but I'll contact the proper authorities and inform them of the situation."

"Look, I'm just letting you know that if I see that thieving Mother F-er around my place again I am gonna decorated his ass with a load of buckshot and someone's gonna have to deal with the dead body." Ole Man Keller rolled up his window and drove off, leaving the officer without his first official bust and wondering if he had made the correct career choice.

## - *Five* -

The television news programming was perpetual in our house. Hank was glued to the local channels for the weather and to the cable stations for world information, but for the most part, he was immersed by political news, which I could care less about. I would rather drink wine until the next election is over. I can't stand the way the programs loop information throughout the day, each time removing it further from the truth. It reminds me of a child's game called "Whisper down the Lane" where children sit in a circle and the first child will whisper a phrase to the next and so on until the whole meaning is lost in translation. Often Hank will come inside the house, flip on the television, and grab a water bottle from the fridge, and then leave with the news program still running. He does this often enough throughout the day that I only need to walk through the room to glean enough sensationalized talking head's regurgitation to know what's going on throughout the planet. It drives me nuts.

The news was loud enough to hear over the running water while washing dishes in the sink. It was the local afternoon show and as usual, I ignored the broadcast until my ears picked up on a motorcycle accident report. Shutting off the water I moved nearer and had a look at the television screen. The Somerville ambulance lights flashed over the broken glass and torn metal remains. Police cars, tow truck and rescue vehicles crammed the scene as the reporter's voice announced the incident, positioned in front of the victim as it rolled on a gurney towards the ambulance. It was easy to surmise the motorcycle driver must have been a man judging by the oversized black biker boots that were left uncovered. A breeze had rippled the white sheet revealing his right arm and what appeared to be a thick black tattoo of a bird on his bicep.

"No way!" I blurted and moved closer to the television to hear.

*"Police report that at eleven forty-five this morning two people were killed in an auto accident. They were traveling on Route Thirteen northbound lanes when the operator of a Harley Davison motorcycle merged into the other vehicle's blind spot while pulling out into the passing lane. Both victims were taken to the county morgue until next of kin are notified."*

"I have to call Walter." I dialed his personal cell. He answered on the first ring.

"What do you want, Molly?"

"Turn on the local news. A guy was just killed on his motorcycle."

"Unfortunately, that happens a lot; they're nothing but death-wish vehicles."

"No Walt, be quiet for a minute. I saw his arm. It had a tattoo of a bird." I couldn't get the words out fast enough.

"So, what is your point?"

"Boy, you are as thick as two short planks sometimes! Don't you see? This could be a lead. We need to go look at his arm."

"Were there any police at the accident?"

"Yes."

"Then they got this." Walter growled and hung up.

"You're such a jackass." I couldn't understand why he didn't find what I said important. What was wrong with him? Didn't he care about that woman at all? Someone has to look into the tattoo, and I guess that someone would be me. I knew what I had to do and reluctantly looked up the number to the county morgue on my phone and dialed. A voice picked up after several rings.

"Somerset County Morgue, how may I help you?"

"Spicer, is that you?"

"Yes, who is this?"

"It's' Molly, Molly Hanson from high school. I need to see you." The connection went quiet. "Hello, are you still there? Why does everyone hang up on me?"

"No, no I'm still here. It's been a while."

"Yes, it has."

"I heard you got married."

"Yes I did. Can I come see you?"

"Are you still married?"

"Yes I am." Oh boy, and I thought this was going to be easy. "I just want to talk. Okay?"

"I'm here until five o'clock."

"All right then, I'll be there in a jiffy." I disconnected the call, ran to my closet and put on a sexier shirt. I checked myself in the mirror and realized I hadn't combed my hair today. I pushed a brush over my head, found my van keys on the kitchen table then left for Somerville.

I couldn't get a date in high school. I wasn't blessed with a pleasing shape like my sister who started her dating career at age twelve. I was gawky, underweight, and flat-chested and if that wasn't enough to doom my high school career, I was taller than the rest of the ninth graders except for Billy Spicer.

Everyone had a date to the freshman prom, everyone apart from for me. Even the girl who repeated the ninth grade three times could secure a date. I suspected Billy's reason for being dateless was because he had one arm that was much longer than the other. Billy lived down the street from my house at the end of horseshoe curve and used the same bus stop as I did. When we were younger children we played together. I never noticed or gave his unevenness a second thought. We would spend our after school hours riding bikes and catching frogs down by the pump house crick. But as the years passed by, puberty had made our friendship weirdly awkward, which caused us to spend the remaining middle and high school years at the bus stop starring at our shoes in silence until one morning in ninth grade when Billy asked me to prom. I unwillingly said yes. Before I could change my mind my mother immediately hauled me downtown to the Sears and Roebuck's dress department to purchase a light baby blue prom dress with embroidered roses. Billy wore a matching light blue tuxedo with dark blue piping and a white ruffled shirt. Photos were taken by both sets of parents before his father drove us to the dance. The evening went wonderfully until the band played the last dance and Billy Spicer tried to kiss me. I pushed him away and ran off to call my mother for a ride home. After that night, Billy and I never spoke again. Until now.

The county morgue was conveniently located behind Hinman's Funeral home on Elm Street. The ride should have taken about twenty minutes but it seemed painfully longer *en route*. Excitement or heartburn spread in my chest at the thought of seeing Billy again, I wasn't sure which. I was thinking hopefully, the trip will be worth it and possibly turn up a lead in the case. Maybe, just maybe then I could help the woman from the water. It's also a possibility that this turns out to be a wild goose chase and I end up stepping knee-deep in goose poop. Maybe I should just go back home right now and act the good wife and clean the house.

I turned off Main Street and pulled into the parking lot. Unsurprisingly there were optimal parking spaces to pick from. The gray cement block building's only bragging rights belonged to a couple of drying half-dead bushes that matched the sad building's exterior. The county really put a lot of thought into this architectural gem.

I checked myself one more time in the rearview and tugged my shirt lower to show a little cleavage before locking up the van. "Good enough."

I was hopeful and walked across the parking lot up the steps to the morgue's glass front doors, took a breath and went inside where Billy Spicer was waiting in the lobby and opened the door for me.

"Hi, Billy."

"Hello, Molly."

"The parking lot is vacant. I didn't think there was anyone here."

"There isn't anyone else, it's just me today. I park around back by the loading area." We stood in each other's presence just as uncomfortable and awkward as in our past. The pregnant pause between us was daunting but familiar and suddenly transported me back in time to that same childhood bus stop.

Billy broke the silence first. "You look like the same Molly Hanson. You haven't changed at all."

"Gee thanks." I wasn't sure if that was a compliment or not.

"No, I mean the same but prettier now."

"And you look different." I almost didn't recognize him. He was more handsome than I remember and wore trendy clothing that actually fit him nicely, masking his unfortunate arm proportioning.

"So what do you want? Why did you want to see me here at the morgue?"

"I need your help with a small matter."

"Tell me. I can't imagine what that would be."

"I'll just say it then. I need you to show me that guy they brought in here this morning, the one from the motorcycle accident."

Billy was slow to answer. I noticed his left eyebrow had twisted upward and it made me feel uneasy.

"Not until you tell me why."

"It's his arm. I need to see if the tattoo matches. It could help in a case I'm working on."

"Who do you think you are, Nancy Drew?"

"I'm serious, can you help me or not?"

"Okay, let me get this straight. You want me to take you down to the basement to look at a dead guy's arm? Now you know I can't do that. It's against regulations. No one but the morgue employees are allowed down there." Billy Spicer started to grin.

"Come on, please? Screw the regulations. There's no one else here. I won't be very long, quick in and out I promise. Please? "

"It will cost you."

"Okay I get it," I said then fished around in my pocket and pulled out a ten dollar bill, a fiver and three ones. The other pocket held forty-three cents and half a pack of Juicy Fruit gum.

"Will this do? "I held out my hands, proudly presenting the loot. Billy's grin had now morphed into a victorious state. He stepped a little closer, examined the total of my pockets cache, and then snatched the money and gum from my hands. "It will do but with one slight condition."

"What's that?"

"We have some unfinished business from a long time ago and I think it's time to pay up. I'll take you downstairs to the basement for the gum and eighteen bucks."

"Great! Let's go."

"Not so fast. There's one more thing."

"Wait, what do you mean by one more thing?"

"I'm still waiting for that kiss."

"What are you talking about? What kiss?" This was going nowhere fast and I was losing patience.

"From a long time ago. You remember that night, on the dance floor. You owe me, Molly." He moved in closer, "You broke my heart."

"Ugh, yes sort of." Recalling that memory had shrunk my posture. I was such a shmuck. "Look, I'm sorry but like you said it was a long time ago. I'll admit it;

I was a big goober back then and I regret running out on you at the dance ever since."

"You should be sorry. I never got over it."

"Can we go downstairs now? I'll be out of your hair in just a few minutes."

"Sure thing, but not without my kiss first."

"You know not! You have got to be kidding me."

"Nope, I'm dead serious and if you want to see the dead guy pay up, it's now or never." Billy closed his eyes and puckered his mouth.

"Oh my God, this is ridiculous." I winced, held my breath then did the deed. "Alright, we're even now, let's go. Take me downstairs."

"Right this way." He exclaimed with more anticipation than a child on Christmas morning.

I followed behind through the heavy gray metal doors and down the stairs that led to the morgue basement until Billy stopped in front of the second set of metal doors with a sign written with red letters warning *No Entry*.

"Are you sure you want to do this?"

"What do you think?" I mocked.

"I see you haven't lost your charm," he said then pushed the auto button and the double doors opened. "Right this way," he gestured his hand for me to go in first.

I stepped inside and glanced around the vast room, "It's pretty chilly in here."

"It keeps the bodies fresh during autopsies, which is a blessing in disguise especially when some are delivered past expiration."

"What do you mean by that?"

"Rank."

"Oh okay, understood. Enough said, it really didn't need further explanation." There was no need to vomit either. My entire digestive organs were twisting from the idea.

The basement room ran the parameters of the building and was partitioned by eight stations with each one containing a table, some sort of apparatuses with tubes, bottle-filled cabinets and various tools with hand cutting saws that sat on the counter next to the sinks. I had no idea the morgue would resemble torture chambers from Hollywood slasher movies. It gave me the willies.

"What's the jar of Vicks for?"

"Like I said, sometimes they come in here already decomposing. A glob of Vicks in each nostril blocks the rancid order."

"Guess you learned that one the hard way."

"No, I learned it in class."

"Wow, you went to school for this? What was the course called, Basics in Gut Jobs 101?" By the look on Billy's insulted face, I may have gone too far. "I'm sorry. I'm a little nervous."

"It's okay. You get used to the jokes in this line of work."

"So what about you? Are you still married?"

"Yeah, twenty two years now," Billy groaned.

"I bet she's proud of you and your big county position." I really needed to see that tattoo. Sucking up at this point would go a long way. God help me, I am so shallow.

"She's not so happy with my work hours. There's many a long night spent down here. I can't do anything about the time of a person's death. I wish she could understand that." Billy looked down at his feet. I suddenly felt a little compassion for his dweebie butt.

"That seems like an excessive amount of tables to me. Do you ever use them all at once?" I can't believe I was coming up with these great questions.

"Sometimes we can get overloaded from a building fire. Car accidents and shootings bring them in by the dozens; any overflow goes up to Salisbury."

"Wow, sounds like complicated hard work." Guess I can add *good liar* to my list of achievements.

"Speaking of which, this is where we store the deceased." Billy pointed over to a wall that was divided, floor to ceiling, by metal doors.

"People are just dying to get in there," he laughed. "Just a little morgue humor, guess you have to work here to get it. As you can see they're refrigerated compartments with removable tables. Here, let me show you." Billy grasped the handle on number 28, and with a slight yank, the table slid out.

"No don't!" I covered my eyes but it was too late.

"It's alright Molly, she's covered up, go on and look."

I cracked my eye open. He was right, the body was covered over with a white sheet. Even though I had it coming, I was beginning to think he was toying with me. "Can you show me the guy who came in this morning, just his right arm please?"

"Sure thing, if I can remember which cubicle I put him in. I think it was this one." Billy reached up to the right side of the wall and opened the door, sliding the table out closer to my face. I fell back a few steps, having never been that close to a dead body before. "I think I just peed."

"Oops, sorry, guess not all of them are covered. That's Mrs. Horowitz. She was brought in yesterday. Here, let me try this one," he said and pulled on a different handle and out came another body.

"That's him I know him by his boots," I was certain the massive man that lay on the table with oversized biker boots still on his feet was the reason for this icky experience. Luckily, the rest of the body was partly covered by a wrinkled sheet.

"He's still dressed. I haven't had time to do anything with him today. I have several ahead of him. Come on around to this side if you want to see his arm." Billy moved out of the way, making room while stretching the man's arm directly under the overhead light. I walked around the table to the other side of the unfortunate deceased and desperately focused my eyes on the fading inky artwork on his stained bicep, searching for an answer. But it wasn't anything like a bird at all, just a Bassett Hound sitting on a ribbon with the words *Daisy Girl* inscribed below. What a buffoon I am, making much to do about nothing.

"Well? What do you think?" He asked.

"That's not it, not even close. I am so sorry I wasted your time, Billy. I should leave now."

"You didn't waste my time. Through all these years you never left my mind. We were good friends once, remember?"

"Yes, I never forgot that." *Liar, liar pants on fire* ran through my head as I left the basement and out to my van. I put the keys in the ignition and pulled away from the parking lot feeling like a big putz. No clues. No matching tattoo. Spooked out by a dead body and kissed a man who wasn't my husband for personal gain. Yep, this was certainly an all-time low.

I drove home much slower, allowing additional time in feeling sorry for myself. I called Hank. I owed him an apology as well.

"Hi honey, where are you? "He asked.

"I am sorry for being such a colossal pain in the butt. Can you forgive me?"

"I don't know what you did this time or what this is about, but I accept your apology for whatever reason. So tell me, what are you up to now?"

"Nothing," I tried sounding convincing. "I'm just in town at the post office picking up some stamps for the house bills."

"Are you okay? You don't sound it."

"Yes I am fine," I said, but nothing could be further from the truth. It was hard to sit in the seat with my tail between my legs.

"Can you stop on the way home?"

"Sure Hank, what do you need?"

"We're out of gravy. "And just like that, all was perfectly right as rain in my world again.

## -*Six*-

Hank was up and gone out to work the water, trying to beat the summer sweltering heat by the time I started moving around sucking down enough coffee to feel like a human being.

Some days I miss my husband more than others, and this certainly was one of those days. He is strong as the earth, with a face that's carved by years of hard work and worry caused mostly by me. His skin is permanently tanned by a lifetime of working in the sun that comes steeped in traditions from the generations that worked their lives on the water before him. And he also cuts a striking figure of a man. Sometimes I will invent an excuse or serious reason to call him at work, even though I know his hands are busy.

It was still early in the day, no different than any other day I pester my husband. I decided to call again.

"What's up, Molly?"

"I was just wondering if you miss me."

"It's hot and I'm a little busy right now pulling pots, I'll call you on the way back, alright?"

"Yes, that's fine." So far the phone call was not rendering the sense of comfort I was seeking.

"Mol?"

"Yes?" Okay, now he'll say the words I need to hear.

"When you let the dogs out, can you check the crab house pump for me? It's a blowout tide and I don't want it sucking minnows or mud into the pipes. I'll be out there all night cleaning up the mess."

"Sure thing hon." Disappointment fell to my feet like a lead balloon. Still, I didn't want to cause him grief. "Will you be out there a long time today?"

"I'm afraid so." Hank finally realized I was having one of those days. "Hey, it's going to be a nice sunset tonight. Why don't we sit out on the pier with a couple of cocktails later on?"

"Sounds perfect." At least I had something to look forward too. Boredom is my number one instigator for trouble.

"I'll be back before you know it." Hank ended the call without the usual *I love you*, proving it was going to be a really long day.

"Come on," I called out and both dogs came trotting through the kitchen. I opened the back door and knocked over a large plastic bag that was left on the steps. Several potatoes, a half jar of mayonnaise, an open bag of cookies, and an orange juice bottle rolled around the sidewalk. "Vegetable Fairy was here again."

This was a common sighting in Smithtown. I know Hank now and then will trade fish for a bag of farm tomatoes, a box of yams or giant zucchinis from an overloaded garden. More often than not it's just food left behind from a weekender, and that is what I had here. I believed it to be a strange ritual stemming from their inability to throw away perfectly good food or just too lazy to take it home with them, as if leaving it on our steps will solve the world hunger problem.

Sara Jane sniffed the bag's contents while Bam peed on a rogue potato. "Now it's my problem," I mumbled, gathering up the mess and tossing it into the trash can on the way to the crab house. The temperature was climbing and would make the water overly warm, causing the crabs to shed fast and bust their shells like popcorn. I placed several soft crabs inside a wire ring to wait a short time. The saltwater hardens their bodies, toughening their new shell enough to skin over. I know people go nuts over devouring a soft shell sandwich but I wouldn't eat one even if you paid me. When a crab sheds his shell, his body is flat and weak with big eyes, like little floating aliens. I couldn't put that in my mouth in a million years.

I arranged the crabs that completed the ideal shed process in the brown wax trays before placing them in the refrigerator and searched though the floats one last time, checking the pump before shutting off the crab house lights. The constant trickling of splashing water streaming from the downspouts and the hypnotizing crabs swimming slowly in zero gravity sent my mind adrift to that morning when the boat hook parted the eelgrass, releasing her form that floated to the surface. Small tears began to well up in my eyes.

"This is absurd. You're tired and need to eat something." I wiped my face and left the crab house, heading back across the yard to the back door and with the dogs pushing past me.

I tossed them a cookie then ferreted through the kitchen cabinets and came across a cherished box of Trix cereal, "Yummy fruity goodness." Reciting the familiar jingle, I piled the colored sugared cereal into a bowl, reached in the fridge only to pick up an empty carton of milk. "This day just gets better and better."

After snatching the van keys I checked myself in the mirror, wiped off a glob of crab goo from my shirt and left the house. Sara jumped in the back while Bam Bam filed into the passenger's side, releasing intestinal pressure.

"You're disgusting," I groaned, quickly turning on the air-conditioning and rolling down the windows until the vehicle's air quality returned to habitable for human consumption. Bam Bam appeared pleased with himself and would smile if he knew how.

We drove through the marsh, past white egrets and cowbirds that poked the mud looking for hidden treasure.

The marsh's beauty comes to an abrupt halt on the last bend by the water tower where the saltwater relinquishes its existence to the freshwater's land. It's an invisible line in the road that hop toads dare never cross in fear of salty skin irritations. The remaining drive to the outside world, where life is unattractive and fast, winds past small communities of depressed housing and the county dump that enlightens the way from paradise until reaching the stoplight entrance to the highway. Annoyed at waiting in the traffic line, I flicked on the satellite radio to get my mind off of my crappy mood. My favorite bluegrass song wafted through the air, the high lonesome melody whined outward from the speaker *"Mothers' not dead she's only a-sleeping, patiently waiting for Jesus to come."*

The song tugged at a memory of last Mother's Day when I had attended a service at the Mennonite Church in Westover. I love the early morning drives to the church through the long tree-lined back roads, passing green farmlands. It usually sets the tone for the morning, but the day was sullied by a steady drizzly rain that made the church dark inside. I remember it smelled like flowers, daffodils, hyacinth, and tulips. I wore cropped white pants and flip flops for the first time since last year. Hank had already been out working on the water for several hours by the time I left the house. I was alone at the service but I was well used to being by myself. Subsequently, it was probably for the better. I was not in the most charming of moods. I hated Mother's Day. It's a Hallmark-induced holiday that only causes my heart to ache.

The church was typically crowded for Mother's Day, one of the few holidays that are driven by guilt.

I spotted a vacant seat up front at the end of the pew by the window. Gazing through the glass pane over at the crooked, vintage headstones that lined the church graveyard, I couldn't help but wonder how many mothers were buried out there beneath the clay, and if they were missed as much as I missed my mother. Although it had been a long time since she passed, the hurt is still palpable and laid heavy on my chest. Her memory brought a sudden lump that tightened my throat. I forced down a swallow, keeping my face angled towards the outside to hide the tears that fell steady like the gray raindrops rolling down the church window. Although I tried leading a decent life, deep down inside lived severe doubt that in my lifetime I will ever become worthy enough to see her again.

My van was second in line and the moment the light turned green the car behind me blasted its horn, which caused the first vehicle to bolt forward. I did the same. Unfortunately, the Chevy Chevette between us didn't move. A sickening crunching sound rose up between our vehicles.

"Oh, you know not!" I jumped out of the van to see if the driver was injured but apparently, he was fine and already heading towards me.

"Are you okay? I am so sorry. The light turned green, I'm sorry."

"You idiot, what kind of moron are you? I was two feet in front of you the whole time, didn't you see me? Where did you get your license anyway, Walmart?" He exploded. Spittle sprayed from his lips. He checked his watch and pulled a cell phone from his pocket. "Thanks to you I'm going to be late." He wore a navy blue a suit that cost more than his car. Probably a lawyer, an ambulance chaser as my fate would have it.

"I said I'm sorry. No need for name-calling."

"I'm calling the police. Look at my car. You ruined it."

"This is asinine; I don't see anything wrong with my car or yours," I insisted, although I did dent his car enough to drive my insurance premium up. I couldn't believe how this day was developing. I should have stayed in bed with the covers over my head.

"You don't see any damage because you're a legally blind moron."

"Please don't call the cops," I pleaded, but it was too late. Whirling dome lights were already flying towards our direction. I'm sure everybody and their mother already called. The squad car was from the Sherriff's office, and only as my luck can roll, Walter stepped from the vehicle.

"Funny, I'm not surprised to see you. What happened here, Molly?" Walter flashed an annoying smirk, removed a small writing pad from his pocket and immediately began writing up our vehicle's tag information.

"We needed milk and gravy."

"Are you injured? How about the dogs?"

"We're fine and so is that irate a-hole. I hit him from a standstill. How much damage can there be?"

"Hold on a minute, what about me? I'm the person that bimbo ran into. You need to take down my statement first."

"Blowhard." I could not stop myself.

"Molly, that's enough out of you." Walter snapped. "I'll get to you in a moment sir, just be patient."

"Sorry, knee jerk reaction," I sighed with my head down.

"What are you talking about, at a standstill?" Walter turned, shielding me from the man with the brim of his hat.

"The light turned green and everybody moved except for Mr. Neanderthal here."

At my expense, Walter smiled into laughter, barely able to document the incident. "Okay, I'll need both your licenses and registrations please." The angry man quickly flashed his credentials in Walter's face.

I searched my van but couldn't locate mine anywhere. "I don't have my license. It must still be at the house. I left in a hurry." Oh God help me. Another violation, higher insurance premiums, and yet again, another disappointment for Hank.

"You should put her ass in jail." The angry man waved his finger at me.

"Please be quiet sir and go wait by your car. I can call a tow truck if you think you need one," Walter calmly replied in monotone syllables to the man who retreated to his vehicle.

In a lowered voice Walt spoke to me. "The Sherriff office is just up the road. We can look up your license on my computer for the report. Just as long as you know I am only doing this as a favor to Hank and not for you."

"I know, thank you, Walt."

"Give me a minute to finish up with this guy then we can go back to my office. I still have to cite you with a driving violation though."

"Oh and I'm sure that just makes your day, doesn't it?"

"I really don't think you are in the position to be snide with me, do you? Pull over to the side of the road and lock up your van. You can ride with me and there's room for your two mutts."

"Okay, thanks." What else could I say at this point?

Walter finished up with the disgruntled motorist then motioned for me to get in the back of the squad car. "Get in."

"Oh, you know not! This is humiliating."

"Yeah ain't it tho?" Walter's mouth curled upward into a satisfied grin. "Gets even better," he said, then flipped on the siren. Bam howled along all the way to the office.

The angry man drove off in a huff as I rode in the cruiser like a criminal, feeling more dented than the Chevette's rear end damage. We pulled into the department's lot and Walt parked the cruiser in a parking spot sporting an official plaque that deemed the space as his and his only. If my parking space had a sign, it would say in bold print *Loser Parking*, under a capital letter *"L."*

"Good time to do this, the office is empty this morning. Most of the employees are on summer holiday, which leaves me short staffed but I like the place to myself. Let's get this over with." Walter locked the cruiser and I followed after him. I didn't lock up my car because nobody in their right mind would ever steal a van. I even left the windows open. Bam Bam would tear a new one in anyone who touched it.

The building was empty like Walt said. Most of the cubicle lights were left off except for his office in the back behind the wooden doors. The furniture décor was severely dated to the eighties but the rest of the office was outfitted with the latest technology. With the ever-growing dissention between us, I had forgotten that Walter is more than my husband's friend and was rather high up in the department's chain of command. I just considered him akin to a root canal dental procedure without Novocain.

"Sure is quiet in here. I appreciate you taking care of this little minor issue for me." Boy, that was really hard for me to say.

"It's not for you, I am doing this is for Hank, remember?" Walter punched words onto his computer's keyboard, scrolling through the department online reporting, "All done."

"That's it?"

"Yep. You'll receive the fine by mail in a few weeks, it's computer-generated now."

"That didn't hurt at all."

"Nope, that comes later when you tell Hank what happened."

"Yes, can't wait," I answered, but his attention had turned to the voice shouting from the reception area. Walter poked his head through the door. "On no, not this idiot again."

"Who is that?"

"He's an official pain in the rear. There are at least twelve complaints called in for petty theft, but we just can't seem to pin a shred of evidence on him. I'm telling you this guy's slicker than snot. I don't understand why we can't catch him in the act. Sit tight, I'll be right back. Now don't touch anything. I mean it, Molly." Walter typed something on his computer that shut the screen down. He left his office and I listened to his footfalls fade down the hall. It only took about a three-second conversation to convince my conscience to open the page.

So what if my moral compass is rusted shut? It's not my fault; Walt should have known better than to leave me alone in his office. I jiggled the mouse to wake up his computer but the screen was locked. "Well I guess you did know better." An empty gray password box remained defiantly on the screen, password required.

I entered Walter's first name, first and last name, and his sheriff name before it dawned on me and typed *Krispy Cream Donut*. Bingo, I was in. Walter had foolishly left several web pages collapsed on the toolbar and I clicked the mouse over the first one. The video game *Candy Crush* loudly popped up which I immediately closed then looked down the hall to see if he was coming. The next web site brought me to deer hunting videos on YouTube. "I'm sure Somerset County would be happy to know Walter was hard at work serving our communities," I whispered then pressed the third collapsed web site.

~ ψ ~

Down the hall in a private beige painted room, an agitated Nate gave his account to Walter at full volume.

"Okay Nate, what is all this commotion about?"

"I want to report some nut bag is threatening to kill me." Nate's face was red and sweaty. His wild eyes bounced around the room. "So are you gonna help me or what?"

Walt took a deep breath before replying, stood up, walked around the table behind Nate, then sat back down in his chair.

"Are you on something right now?"

"No."

"You sure? You're acting like it."

"Yeah man, I'm sure. I don't have no money for that."

"Alright then, tell me what happened from the beginning." Walter sighed and rubbed his eyes as Nate told his story, speaking without a breath, comma or period, just one big run-on sentence.

"I was driving into Rumbley Harbor when I saw Ole Man Keller sitting outside smoking a cigarette, and like I said I have no funds so I stopped and asked him for one, and he said he didn't have any for me but had one lit in his hand and in the other hand he had a beer so I asked him for one of those and he said no he didn't have none for me and I said come on I know you got one for me and he said he was out, which I didn't believe him so I went in his house and got one from the fridge. He cussed at me and chased me off the property so I went next door again cause I knew someone was home but no one answered the door for a while and by then, my beer was empty so I came back across the grass and went and got another beer cause it was hot out and all. That's when he threatened to kill me real loud like. See what I mean, he was wrong about the beer."

"Nate?" Walter leaned back in his chair.

"Yeah?"

"Do you like to fish, Nate?"

"What are you talking about? Man, you crazy. I just told you some dude wants to kill me and you ask me about going fishing?"

"I like to fish, I find it soothing. Some days I catch that big one and some days I don't, but I always catch a fish. Do you know why, Nate?"

"No, why? "Nate studied Walter's face, given there wasn't one reason to trust him.

"Because fish ain't that smart. They think they are but eventually grab onto that bait. They kinda remind me of you. Do you know what I mean, Nate?"

"No, I don't know what you're talking about, man."

Walter shook his head, letting out another deep desperate breath. "I tell ya what, if you'd like, I'll drive on out to Rumbley and have a talk with Mr. Keller, although he will most likely press charges for trespassing and unlawful entry."

"No man, don't do that." Nate stood up and so did Walter.

"Just as I thought, guess you'll be going now?"

"Yeah man, I'm gone," said Nate, leaving for the exit.

"Oh, and by the way, Nate?"

"Huh?"

"Why don't you do us all a favor and take up residence out of state?"

Nate stormed out the door without responding. Walter shook his head again then returned down the hall to his office door and turned the knob.

~ ψ ~

I opened the last file collapsed on the computer's toolbar to see a mug shot of a man. His face was pretty, the kind of face that let him get away with anything. Though I had never seen his face before, I recognized the name. Nathan J. was listed at the top of the file. Skimming through a mile long list of petty arrests, I opened the next tab showing evidence photos from the array of offenses and my eyes fell on one in particular of Nate with two half-naked, tatted up young women. He sat on a black Harley Davidson motorcycle with each of the girls sexually flanking his legs. Several of the photos displayed the girls in different suggestive poses. They appeared to have been at a large wooded area, probably a biker party. There was something odd in the photos that struck me besides the fact that they were obviously missing pertinent clothing and stoned out of their gourds. It was the woman straddling Nate's left leg who wore very expensive sandals, the preppy leather kind that tie above the ankle. Her hair was perfectly coiffed and her nails were pink manicured. Why would an upper-class girl like that be naked and high at a biker party? I wondered if it was it by her own choice, but addiction doesn't discriminate by class.

"Molly, what the hell are you doing? That's official business, how did you even get into my computer?" Desperate to shut down the screen Walter tried seizing the computer mouse from my hand, which quickly turned into a wrestling match knocking it onto the floor. I dove for the mouse but Walter kicked it across the room. This was going nowhere fast.

"Stop," I bellowed. "Wait a minute. Did you see this photo? Look at her shoes." Yanking on his arm I drug him back to the computer and pointed to the screen.

"Oh, I've already seen that file. It's over a week old."

"It's the girl, look closer. She's wearing very pricey shoes and look at her hair. Don't you find her a little out of place? Just one look and you can tell she's from some high dollar neighborhood. Why would she be hanging with dregs of society?"

"We already know all this, Molly. She's been reported missing." Walter closed the computer screen.

"Wait, what? She's missing? When? Do you think this guy could be involved?"

"Forget about it Molly, the state police already had him in for questioning but there isn't any evidence linking him to the case."

"What about his friend Victor? What happened to him?"

Walter stopped his protest and rubbed his chin carefully thinking about what he was about to say. "He died."

"Don't you think I know that?"

"But how do you know, that is the question."

"Never mind that and tell me what the cause of death was? Was he a good friend of this guy, Nate?"

"The keyword here is *was*. He died from affixation."

"He was murdered?"

"We don't know. Evidence from the autopsy was inconclusive. There was a high level of alcohol in his system. His drunken ass could have fallen in the ditch, passed out with the tide coming up and that was all she wrote."

"But," is all I managed to say before he cut me off.

"Stay out of the way and leave this to the police Molly, you have bigger fish to fry anyway. Wait until Hank finds out you banged up your van."

There is nothing more in this world I hated than when Walter was right. I closed my eyes and lay my face in my hands. "By now I can guarantee he already knows."

## - *Seven* -

Seven mornings ago at zero-dark-thirty in the morning, the air was absent from any sound; only the trickle of water that flowed under River Road's cement bridge could be heard. It was the darkest hour, just before dawn when the light waited in stillness up to that last moment as the night surrenders to the day. Stones pinched and flew off under the tire's weight, reverberations piercing the silence as a vehicle slowly appeared, rolling onto the bridge. Brake lights beamed as the car came to a stop mid-way. A door opened with a single interior light illuminating a figure that climbed out from the car. It moved around to the back of the car, dimmed by the dark as it struggled with a bulky sack from inside the trunk. A sudden thud splashed the water followed by the closing of a car door, leaving the bridge once again in darkness as the vehicle drove away the same as it came, quietly vanishing into the early blackness.

## *-Eight -*

I noticed the figure of a woman standing at the end of our pier. Although I didn't recognize her, I figured she must be a neighbor's relative or friend. Nobody here minds if someone walks out on their pier. I shouldn't either. Judging by her clothes and her small, thin frame I would say she was between eighteen to twenty years of age. She appeared to be photographing scenery and anything else that moved before her through the marsh, from herons in the ditch to fiddler crabs and a sailboat heading upriver. That made me chuckle because Hank always said he would rather have a sister in a whore house than have a brother with a blow boat. Must be a waterman thing.

I couldn't look away from the girl; she was so enthralled by the island as if really seeing it for the first time. I was just like her once, back when Hank and I were first married. The island's environment was so strange to me it was a difficult adjustment, unforgiving and stunningly beautiful at the same time. I was suddenly isolated from the outside world and yet shunned by the locals for years. I had learned the hard way that a *Come Here* was viewed with such disdain as if my presence threatened the islander's very existence, as if I had become a stain on their precious heritage. Eventually, after a long time of proving my salt worth, I became tolerated akin to an invasive species, and blended with the salty air that absorbs into my lungs, and my blood.

I have become part of the landscape and unnoticed by its wildlife. I never in a million years could have imagined I would be living my life around weather patterns, high tides or seasons on the Tangier Sound, and most of the time I'm not hardy enough for this crap.

I went to the kitchen and poured a bowl of fruit colored sugary cereal then reached in the fridge for milk. "You have got to be kidding me." I never did buy that milk yesterday.

Continuing my food mission I looked through the cabinets for something else to fill my gut and found two packs of chicken-flavored Ramen Noodles, an empty peanut butter jar and rediscovered we were low on gravy. Not even a can of tomato soup to be found. I thought the fridge and freezer held a possibility for something edible to eat only to strike out there as well. "How could this be?" Another startling realization about me had just occurred: I really sucked at being a housewife. I knew I had to put on my big girl panties and go shopping for groceries. But I also sucked at shopping.

Before going off the island, I let the dogs out, tossed them each a cookie and patted their hairy heads goodbye. I know that, as dogs, they cannot tell the amount of time I have been MIA, but still I felt guilty for ditching them.

I opened the van door and was instantaneously greeted by a blast of heat to the face. The morning sun had begun to steam Smithtown to a humid ninety degrees where it would remain unbearably sticky hot until mid-October. I set the van's air conditioner temperature to iceberg, relieved when it hissed cool air through the vents. My van is very old and has rusty chunks that randomly fall off in the driveway. When it rains, it leaks liquid rust, leaving the carpeted floor resembling a murder scene. Thumbtacks hold the ceiling material in place and the last time I had the oil changed, the computerized manufacturer maintenance manual suggested that at this point, I should seriously consider buying a new car and sell this one for scrap metal. I don't care what anybody says, I'm keeping the van until the doors fall off, which could be any minute now.

The drive leaving Smithtown that winds through the marsh and over the three bridges is only about a four-mile stretch. On my left a doe drank from a freshwater pond as a Great Blue Heron fished near her. It's wild and untouched and has gone unnoticed by advancing time with only a thin road that connects between two worlds.

I slowed the van to a stop, got out and helped a turtle to the other side. On hot and muggy days the summer heat signals female terrapins to leave the bay and lay their eggs on the shore in the softer, sandy dirt. Unfortunately, many will come to their demise smashed under vehicle tires. The latest rumor is that some watermen will run turtles over on purpose. I don't know if all that's really true, but I do know people are very scary behind the wheel. Due to her accumulated age, my friend Sylvie had terrified me on several occasions while driving. She never cared for the phrase senior and would often refer to herself as a seasoned citizen. I sure miss her and her oversized ugly brown car. For a short while, Sylvie was the only friend I knew, and in a roundabout way, she could keep my insanity at bay. Our friendship was odd and at times strained by her stubborn wisdom which she insisted was the right and only way. Despite myself, I still learned a good many things about life from her. She had a way of getting in and out of trouble with ease and came and went just as unexpectedly from my life, leaving behind an emptiness as familiar as my parent's death. She also left behind her brown bomber which I drove the crap out of until a raccoon ran out in the road and I ended up in the ditch at high tide. That was the end of Sylvie's car. If she was still alive today I can guarantee she would still be chewing my ass out for totaling her car.

I heard my cell phone ring from inside the van and hurried back to answer and picked up on the last ring. "Hello, you still there?"

"Hi hon, you sound out of breath." It was Hank.

"I am a little. I was saving another turtle."

"Good. That's why I was calling. I was hoping you were laying low today and staying out of trouble for a change."

We never did discuss my accident last night. Hank was too tired and I certainly didn't want to bring it up in conversation. I knew Walter would tell him the first chance he had but I didn't think Walter told him about what I found on his computer. Guess I owed Walt one and that's really unfortunate for me.

"Just heading out to grocery shop at Walmart," I said starting up the van.

"Did you put me on speaker?" Hank asked.

"Of course," I refuted then quickly switched over to blue tooth.

"Molly please, don't go to Walmart today, you know it never ends well for you. Turn around and go home," he pleaded, hoping to convince me. I was thinking, I don't know what his problem is. It's not like I'm going to be hit over the head with a garden shovel, hogtied and left for dead propped up against a meat freezer. What are the chances of that happening twice?

"It will be fine. You're fretting for no reason. I'll be a quick in and out. Besides, I'm already halfway there, just passing by that naked guy's house." I never did understand why, but there is a man who prefers to get dressed and undressed in his driveway. Hank says he does that because he works at the Perdue chicken plant.

Hank also said it's not for us to judge people because in the end is when we all will be judged and that it takes all kinds to make the world go around. The only cool factoid I can refer too is *This ain't no dress rehearsal so better have all the fun now while you still can.* Too bad I'm not half the man my husband is.

"Mol, why don't you try and remember for a minute everything that has happened to you at Walmart. I think that might change your mind about going there."

Okay, as usual, he was right as rain. "There was that time when Bam Bam took off across the parking lot, dodging cars then made his way into the store where I chased him around for an hour. That was Bam's fault, not mine."

"What about when you broadsided the State Police car? And that time knocked down the entire paper goods aisle last year? Have you forgotten about that? "

"It was a misunderstanding and you know that." God has tested my faith many times in many ways and I believe if I can make it through a Walmart shopping trip just one time without a public incident, then and only then I will be allowed through heaven's pearly gates.

"You had six months' probation!" Hank snapped. "Everyone knew about what you did, it was embarrassing. "Hank's volume cranked up a notch.

"The Somerset County court system has forgiven me, why can't you?"

"I forgive you every single time. I wish I didn't have to do it so often."

"I know, I know, you don't have to lecture me. I have a short shopping list, I won't be long. I promise."

"I think I'm getting a stomach ulcer." Hank groaned into the receiver. Even though I couldn't see him I'm sure he threw his arms up in defeat.

"I love you," I stated, hoping those three little words would diffuse my husband's frustration.

"Do you have gravy on the shopping list?"

"Yes, I wrote it down."

"Then I love you too." Hank disconnected the call, still unnecessarily worried about me. What could possibly go wrong? As with the immortal spoken words by Popeye, I am what I am.

The Walmart parking lot was fairly empty when I rolled in, hopefully a good omen. I pulled into the closest space I could find and told myself walking around the store would be enough exercise for the day. I shoved the list in my pocket and pressed the key lock on the van.

"As if someone would steal that piece of crap," chuckled a man sitting in the car next to me.

"Hey, I heard that, and it was rude, you know."

"Your car is an offensive eyesore."

I was about to flip him the bird then remembered what Hank said on the phone and instead lowered my hand to my side, turned around and walked towards the entrance. Boy, that hurt, I'm not used to that sort of self-control.

Inside, the store's neon lighting stunned my eyesight making it difficult to read my list. There was no need to hurry so I took my time filling the shopping cart with a gallon of milk, a bag of cheesy poofs, potato chips, a box of chocolate ding dongs, and six jars of gravy. I had everything we needed except pizza and French fries. Just to be on the safe side I skipped the spaghetti-O aisle and moved on towards the frozen food area of the store, scanning the frosty doors for the last of the items.

I'm not sure if I heard the stinging snickers or felt their burning gaze first as the murmur of laughter rose behind me. I pretended not to notice, but from the corner of my eye, I could see it was Linda Lawrence and Colleen Bookman from Hank's high school days.

"Aw, you know not, it's the evil bitches of Crisfield High," I shuddered. Snarly ridiculing voices instantly transported through time to when I was an ugly adolescent duckling. There are moments in everyone's life when scars permanently stain our soul, and there they will remain a constant reminder of ugliness. It was at Hank's high school reunion when I was introduced to two of life's blemished examples. A couple of alcoholic drinks later had encouraged the flirty pair to become a little too hands-on with my husband. Now, normally I would consider myself to be nonconfrontational by nature and prefer to take the *Duck and Run* approach, but... Let's just say that the evening didn't end on a good note after I poured my cocktail down the front of Linda's dress followed by a few choice words. After that night, Hank would go to his future high school reunions without me.

For a fast escape, I turned my cart around but was blocked in by other shoppers unaware of the impending doom. The menacing duo moved in closer for the kill, evaluating the contents in my cart and then critically wounded their prey.

"Well, well, well, if it isn't Molly Hanson, acting just like the perfect little housewife. I see you're quite the chef, whipping up gourmet meals for that handsome husband of yours, I see."

Shrills of wicked laughter bounced between the freezer's frozen glass. Just to make her point, Linda lifted high a bag of frozen fries from my cart then dramatically let fall to the ground, splitting the bag open. Fries spilled across the aisle. I wanted to throw up.

"My, my, do you think you have enough gravy?" Colleen laughed in unison with Linda, screeching to a sonic pitched noise.

"Poor Hank, it's a real shame. Why he should have known better than to marry a *Come Here*." A wretched smile stretched across her mouth.

There was once a time in my life when I would have hauled off and punched them both in the tits, but as I mature over the years I try to put the wisdom I have learned the hard way to good use and render better behavior on my part. I hate it when that happens, but for my husband's sake, I decided to take the high road.

"Yeah well if it wasn't for us *Come Here's* you all would be nothing but a bunch of ignorant inbred morons turning out potato chips for children." I grinned, picked up the ripped bag of fries from the floor, swapping them for an unopened bag, and proudly flipped the bird in one fell motion. Victorious at last, I left Hank's malevolent groupies dumbfounded in the frozen foods section. "Score one for the nerd," I shouted and headed towards the checkout, feeling pretty pumped until I came upon the long lines that waited for me. Every lane was crowded, including the express lane. It's understood that an inordinate amount of time will be spent standing in a checkout line but today was ridiculous.

"I should have packed a sandwich," I moaned loud enough for the checkout attendee to hear and shoot me a look.

The biggest problem with standing in line is I start thinking, and too much alone time in my head never ends well. Doubt flooded my mind. Although it felt good at the time, I could have handled the bitches differently and walked away with dignity instead of stooping to their level. Possibly everything they said was true and Hank could have done a lot better than me. Maybe he should have married someone else, someone special that would make him proud instead of embarrassed. I felt like crap. Sweat formed on my brow.

"I'm dying here." The line hadn't budged an inch. I was boxed in with no hope of escape and my blood was starting to boil. Bordering on a complete mental meltdown, I needed to focus, and kept my eyes entertained by the woman ahead of me in line. The back of her tank-topped shoulder sported a purple unicorn. Seriously, I don't get it. Why bother to endure that much pain for such a silly image? Get a battleship sprawled across your chest. Go big or go home.

"I got to get out of here before I commit Hara-kiri," I cried, squeezing past the shoppers. Abandoning the shopping cart in the checkout line, I quickly hoofed it back to my van.

"It will be a miracle if that thing starts up." The rude man was still sitting in his car. I couldn't believe it. What's up with this guy? He was baiting me but I wasn't putting up with that and had my fill of rotten people for one day.

"Oops, so sorry." I rammed the van door into the side of his shiny sedan sized vehicle, deeply denting the door.

"What the hell lady? Are you nuts?"

"Mean people suck," I hollered out the window, put the van in reverse and roared out of the lot spraying his car with stones. Maybe I was wrong, and now my entrance to heaven will be once again delayed, but it was worth it.

I drove onto the highway, ignoring the turnoff for the Crisfield/Smithtown points and continued in the northbound lanes towards Salisbury. I was going to find the place that Walt had sent a photo of the tattooed bird from the woman in the water's back. How many tat salons could there be anyway? I decided to come up with a plan and pulled over to the side of the road to look up the locations of Salisbury tattoo parlors on my phone, scrolling through the long list of tat shops.

"Let's see if I can remember which one it was. There's a shop over on Broad and West Street, *Needle Point Tattoos*. Nope that ain't it. On north thirteen near the mall is the *Tattoo Temple*. No, that's not it either. *INKspirations Body Art,* now that's just plain silly." I was about to give up when I came across a name that sounded familiar. The *Blue Moon Tattoo* parlor sat a couple of doors down from the Roller Derby Rink and Martial Arts Center. I have been known to frequent the women's roller derby league matches. Truth be told, I have secretly desired to be a Salisbury Roller Girl, but I'm too much of a wuss to try out for the league. Shame really, I had even created my very own derby tag name, *Dudley Do Wrong*.

Twenty minutes later I was sitting in front of the Blue Moon Tattoo. A red neon sign blinked *Open*, which would be really convenient if I needed a tat done during lunch hour. Too bad the rink wasn't running. I would rather be inside eating cheese fries and watching outrageous women on roller skates whirl around the rink punching into each other. It's an honorable sport.

Another twenty minutes went by as I worked up the nerve to go inside the tat shop. My stomach churned with every anxious pang, or maybe I was just hungry from thinking about those cheese fries. The other possibility could be my brain telling me this was a stupid idea and I should go home immediately. Ignoring all common sense, I marched my big girl panties through the Blue Moon Tattoo's glass door.

"You want tattoo?" inquired a fellow sporting a Fu Man Chu mustache and a heavy Asian accent. He was standing by an overstuffed velvet maroon red chair marred by cigarette burns and motioned for me to sit with his ink-stained fingers that held a long skinny cigarette. "You wait here. I make your tattoo soon. You next, I have someone first. Look at pictures on wall for inspiration. I can do anything you like," he said, inhaling on his cigarette. I coughed, waving at the air. He tilted his head in contemplation before taking another puff. "So, you don't look like the tattoo type." He was easing off the fake accent.

"It's my birthday and I wanted to mark the occasion," I announced, surprised how easy it was to lie to him.

"Oh, I see. Important year for you?"

"Yes, I am celebrating the big four-o."

"Hmm, I thought you much, much older." He turned around, disappearing behind a beaded curtain. As he switched on the tattoo gun, a buzzing sound bled between the beads. Fu Man Chu began working on a man's forearm, occasionally wiping blood away, returning the needled gun to his skin and repeated the process causing the tattoo recipient to wince each time. Gray white smoke lingered in a halo around his head. My stomach was nervous and the wooziness caused my palms to perspire. I needed to pull myself together and concentrate on the mission. "I am looking for something specific I've seen before, like a bird." I spoke loud enough for Fu to hear me over the inking gun.

"We have birds, look at pictures."

I did what he told me to do. Hundreds of photographs lined the walls. Intricate artwork proudly displayed on flesh, each design personal to the new owner. I didn't see what I was looking for but it helped take my mind off the painful procedure occurring behind the beads. I carefully examined the wall until settling on one photo in particular. It was of a man showing off his newly tattooed pumped bicep. The photo was taken in the parking lot with the Blue Moon Tattoo storefront in the background. He was sitting on a Harley motorcycle low rider with fat tires. I focused on his face and my breathing quickened when I recognized it was Nate perched on the motorcycle.

"Okay we all done, you ready? You know what you want?" Fu Man Chu stepped out from the curtain with his tattooed client following behind, stopping to check his new arm ornament in the mirror. Why didn't I notice before that he was a biker when a decent percent of the tattoo clientele make up the demographic? Our eyes locked in the mirror and I panicked.

"I changed my mind, I'm sorry I have to go now," I stammered, pushing by them both and running out of the door. With trembling hands, I managed to get the keys in the ignition, start the van and peel out of the parking lot.

My wits had returned by the time the adrenaline dissipated from my body. I was calmer, thinking much clearer now. I needed to tell Walter about Nate's photograph and reluctantly dialed his cell.

"Wait what? You were where? What were you thinking, Molly? Are you telling me you have a tattoo now? Oh boy, Hank is really going to flip his lid this time." Walt was shouting.

"No wait, I didn't do it," I tried to explain but Walter cut me off.

"There has to be something seriously wrong with you. Why do you find it necessary in making such asinine decisions, one after another?"

"Why won't you listen to me for just once?"

"No, Molly. What goes on in this or any other police office is none of your business. Go ahead, keep up these shenanigans and you'll find yourself spending time in a six by six cell with a roommate named Big Bertha. Oh, and I can guaran-damn-tee Hank will leave your sorry butt in there this time."

I could hear Walter's blood pressure rising through the receiver and figured it was not the time for a snappy retort. Hank would be pretty upset with me if I caused the cardiac arrest that killed off his friend. I resisted using my favorite moniker *Jerk Face* that's reserved for Walter and waited until his breathing slowed. "I'm sorry Walt. I just wish I could help her."

Walter knew who I was talking about, even though he only shows passion when it comes to a jelly glazed donut. I guessed her murder probably weighed as heavily on his mind as it did on mine, or almost.

"Do you even know what time it is? You know Hank will be home soon from another hard day of work. Why don't you go home and be a good wife to him, bake a cake or anything else that resembles normal behavior." Click. He hung up on me again.

I eased the gas pedal down and drove my sorry ass home, thinking I should be back well before Hank, in time to have his coffee ready. Too bad I don't know how to make a cake. The only thing I use the oven rack for is storing wine bottles.

By the time I reached home, Hank was already at the house and pouring a cup of coffee when I walked into the kitchen. "Hi hon, what did you get into today?" he looked up and beamed a smile.

"Nothing really, why, what did you hear?" Good lord, why did I say that? I knew I don't need Hank's approval and yet guilt reigned over my conscience.

Hank shook his head then opened the fridge door to fetch the milk for his coffee. "I thought you said you were going to Walmart to buy milk today?"

I smacked my forehead in response, realizing that my flight to heaven may be on an extended holding pattern.

## - *Nine* -

The temperature was perfect. A gentle soothing wind generated a small breeze through the opened bedroom window, its lazy sheer panel defiantly moving in compliance. It was still cool enough to sleep without sticking to the sheets but it was early and the sun would soon scorch the tiny island with its blasting rays. In Smithtown, any habitable weather is brief and I was enjoying what was left of the morning on the deck with my canine companions. The air held less than its usual humidity load for a change. I expected a good hair day for me. I had manageable hair before I moved here, before it was whipped into knots by relentless winds that can blow furniture clear off the island. Even the local beauty salon's hair damaging devices will never compare to the force of Smithtown's blasts.

Today the Tangier Sound was quiet and clear across the water and flat enough to blend the horizon into the sky. Out past the buoy markers where the water runs deep were dolphins rounding up a school of bunker. Out on the sound, threatening storm clouds are visible before the weather radio alarm can announce a warning. Often a patchy rain cloud will spray the air into a florescent prism. The watermen call that a *Sun Dog*. "Bad weathers' coming in," they say at its sighting.

I could hear Hank's boat engine fade to a stop, then a clanking noise began and echoed into the air as he drove the bank trap poles down into the black mucky mud bottom, repeating the process at each set and moving on to the next. I had been fortunate enough to observe the curiosity of otters first hand when I help Hank set gear in the water. They swim through the poles, obsessively touching each one, and follow Hank up the creek after each finished set. Nervous compulsive behavior appears to be second nature in otters.

Sara Jane and Bam were snoozing in the breeze by my feet. I reached down and massaged Sara's soft velvet ears. Bam rolled over, yawing with his spotted black tongue, stretched and let out gas.

"Tell me again why we brought you home when there were so many other cute little dogs I could have chosen from?" I remember the day we met him at the pound. It was difficult to walk down the hall, passing by all the more desirable dogs. We found Bam Bam housed outside across the pound yard all alone in a kennel. It was his last chance before euthanization. I didn't want a second dog but Hank insisted and had owned cattle dogs in the past. We knew Bam's time was running short and decided to change the dog's destiny that day and brought home the furry mess, intestinal distress and all.

A large bird flew overhead that distracted Bam and set him off running in his usual fit. A male osprey scanning the water for nourishment needed for his chicks waiting in their nest at the end of the neighbor's pier. Meanwhile, the female's high pitched chirp beckons him to hasten. His hunt will end successfully with a fish clutched in his claws. Each year the pair chooses a new nesting location; their ritual marks the beginning of spring, sometimes settling on a different pier, telephone pole or a skeleton crab shack that's past its prime. Nature is so divine in its process between mating pairs of animals with a loyalty that never waivers, unlike humans, especially in the male species. A man's self-importance is immeasurable. With every year he grows more chivalrous in virtue but will easily betray his partner with a glance, a casual flirtation, and sometimes even an affair. After all, his virility is at stake. *Most men, anyway.*

The osprey's voice screeched against the sky. I have come to know many of the shore birds by sound and can imitate several varieties, including the tundra swans that winter over on the islands. There are so many wonderful living things on the island, gifts that fill your eyes with pleasure. Smithtown has an owl that I have never seen but I call him in the night and he replies out of curiosity. These are the few moments that can make life bearable on the island. It's the raw beauty that I appreciate the most, until a greenhead bites your skin. I swatted the pesky invader from my leg. God must have a sense of humor.

Why else would he have created an annoying creature that can tear flesh from your bones?

The time was well past due for fishing up the soft crabs. I hurried back to the shanty, Bam jogging up behind me while Sara remained asleep on the deck. I ran through the usual routine of checking clogged pipes, dipping the net through the water, and gently lifting newly formed soft crabs into a wire ring to finish fluffing their bodies to full size. It's the most vulnerable moment for the female crab in open waters. A male will secure a hold on a female crab, or *she-crab*, throughout the shed process, breeding her until the saltwater hardens her shell. I used to find the whole process fascinating the first five thousand times I saw it.

In the refrigerator, I placed a tray full of soft crabs on the shelf, ignoring the jacked up truck that rolled by the house. It was common for a few cars to pass by, sometimes stopping in to chat a bit with comfortable authority about the state of the current crabbing market. Often just a friendly wave as they went by. And it was that time of day when the boats offload their catch, so why would I have given any attention to the trucks driving up and down Smithtown Road or pay any mind to the truck that parked in our oyster shell driveway or notice the man standing at the crab house doorway?

"Where's Hank? I need some dead peelers for bait, going fishing on the second bridge," his voice demanded.

"I'm sorry, didn't hear you come in." I about jumped out of my skin. It's common for people to stop by for a bushel of crabs; I should be used to it by now.

"Where's Hank? Is he still out there?" the voice asked again. I couldn't tell who it was, his figure shadowed by the sunshine. He could be anyone of the many who came to purchase seafood from the crab house. Hank often forgets to inform me when someone is scheduled for a pick-up and I get stuck dealing with people and scooping up the bushels of angry grabs.

He stepped inside under the strands of bare light bulbs and there was no mistaking his face. It was the same face as on the rap sheet photo from Walter's computer. Nate's eyes darted around the crab house making a mental list of anything valuable to retrieve at a later date.

"Yes, he's still on the water but he'll be pulling up and minute now." I felt my pockets for my phone, realizing I left it in the house and swallowed hard, cursing myself for not having it. Bam had a bead on Nate as he moved steadily closer. I backed up a few steps but Nate moved in, pinning me against the refrigerator. His hand lay flat against the metal door next to my head as he spoke his hot breath on my face.

"It's a low down dirty shame leaving a pretty woman like you all alone in this cool dark crab house where no one can see or hear you." Caressing his fingers through my hair he parted a smile showing his meth mouth with rotten teeth from heavy drug use. My heart began to pound loudly in my ears. Sensing danger Bam butted between us uttering a low growl. Nate kicked at him and Bam spun around in one swift move and nipped the back of Nate's calf, blood seeped through the jeans.

"Hey, what the hell, that dog bit me!" He bellowed in pain backing away from us both.

"Good dog," my voice gave way to a tremble. "With another word from me, he'll tear you a new one. I think its best you leave now before he rips your head off. Go away and leave me alone." I pulled Bam Bam in and held my arms tight around his neck. Nate examined the bite on his leg, lifted the bucket full of crab sheds, backed out of the crab house without removing his empty glare from either of us, and drove away from Smithtown in his jacked up truck. I ran to the floats out back, watching in relief as he departed down the road, across the marsh and out of sight from Smithtown.

"Oh, come here good boy." I bent down and hugged the cattle dog hero who returned the affection by licking my face. "Okay, okay that's enough. Come on let's go in the house and call Hank."

My phone was sitting on the kitchen table right where I left it. Oddly, there was a missed call notice from Hank. I was still distraught and needed to pull myself together before calling, but dialed his number anyway. "Hank I'm sorry I was in the crab house when you phoned me."

"Hi hon, what's the matter, you sound a little upset? Is everything alright?" Apprehension hung thick in his voice. "Molly? Answer me."

"Yes, yes I'm alright," I could barely utter a syllable. Tears broke down my cheeks.

"Molly, tell me what's wrong? I'm coming home right now, I'll be there as soon as I can," Hank shouted over the boat's noisy engine.

"It was that guy Nate; he was here in the crab house. I'm probably just overreacting but he scared the life out of me. I'm fine now." The adrenaline that had coursed through my veins a few moments ago left me weakened and sobbing into the phone.

"What do you mean? Did he hurt you? If that idiot touched even one little strand of hair on your head I'll kill him dead. I swear I will."

"No, no I am okay, really I am."

"I'm almost home. Calm down, everything will be alright."

~ ψ ~

Hank pushed the throttle forward, stressing the boat to its limit. The hull banged atop waves, toppling crab baskets and sending them rolling around the deck as it sped dead on for the small pier that runs from the crab house to the crick. His hands were clutched, digging his fingers into the hard rubber steering wheel cover. An angry fear curled up his spin knowing what Nate was capable of. Pulling up to the wharf in high speed and sprayed mud up over the marsh, Hank quickly tossed the ropes over the cleats then ran past the crab house and through the back screen door.

~ ψ ~

I was on the kitchen floor huddled against the base cabinet. Hank grabbed my shoulders, lifting me up with both of his hands. It kinda hurt.

"I'm fine, really I am." The terror across his face made me sick knowing I was responsible.

"Please tell me you are okay?"

"Yes, I told you I am, just a little shaken that's all. The whole thing was weird and scary." I tried sounding brave.

"Did he touch you?"

"Only my hair. Like I said, it was weird. He enjoyed toying with me. It was intimidating..."

"I'm gonna kill him."

"No Hank, he didn't actually do anything wrong, just scared me that's all. I feel a little foolish for being so upset."

"He shouldn't be anywhere near our home or in my crab house. I'm reporting this to Walter." Hank left the kitchen with both of his fists tightly balled into a wad. He paced the front yard whirling his arm in the air during the call, and in true form, I pressed my ear to the window listening in on their conversation.

"No, he didn't hurt her, frightened yes, but that's all he did except for making off with a bucket of peeler shell sheddings. I don't care about that bucket, he can have the whole stinking thing. I'm telling you, Walt, if he ever comes here again, it won't end pretty."

I couldn't hear what Walter on his end of the line, but by Hank's tone throughout the conversation, I came to the conclusion that nothing can or will be done about Nate. I shivered at the thought.

"No Walt, he didn't steal crabs or anything else, they were already dead. Okay, yeah she's fine, uh-huh, yep, thanks man. Yes, understood." Click. Hank had positioned himself firmly in the yard with hands on his hips. I came outside and slipped my arms around his waist. "What's going to happen now?"

"Walt said he'll take care of it." Hank put his arm over my shoulder, and the tension let go of my body.

"I said I'm fine, you know. Don't worry so much about me."

"I try, Molly. Lord knows I try not to worry," he sighed.

I didn't know what to do about what happened with Nate in the crab house, and I was sure Hank was thinking the same thing. Nate's presence was strong and standing between us. I searched for the words that would fix this deafening silence but only proved the effort futile. I remained holding onto his arm as a light wind teased through my hair. The sun shifted lower in the sky dissolving its changing color into the water. Hank squeezed my hand. "I'm sorry, I should have been here."

"You would have killed him."

"I know."

## -*Ten* -

"You coming to bed or what?"

"Be there in a minute." Who was I kidding? I knew damn well there would be zero sleep for me tonight, not after the horrendous day I had, and the second glass of wine I was drinking had minimal effect on consoling my nerves. It was too bright to sleep anyway with that glaring super moon lighting the evening sky like it was high noon. It was annoying but pretty spectacular to see.

I stepped out into the night, glass of wine in hand, and moseyed down two hundred feet out over the water to the end where our wooden fishing pier narrows. I sat down at the edge and dangled my legs over the water, enjoying the rest of the chardonnay. Usually, no one can see me out here but tonight my shaded image outline was sharpened by the brilliant moonbeams.

Listening to the wildlife rustling at night is a different experience than during the day. It resonates clearer the longer I listen, more beautiful than the symphony's crescendo as if it has let down its guard and accepted my presence. Hank always makes it into bed early and does not know I come out here after nightfall. Too bad he misses the night's splendor, the stars so near and heavy and the conversation of waves capping in a blind movement.

From the pier, I noticed most of the lights in the Smithtown houses are turned off. Funny how in Smithtown there's a whole lot of nothing going on, and yet I can manage to be real busy at it. The moon's reflection danced and wiggled on the water. Its pull will probably flood the roads by the morning. Being kept off-island from high water is almost as bad as being marooned on it. I remember someone once said they lost their car keys, giving them great cause for concern they'd be trapped in Smithtown forever. I think they were only joking but I have my car keys and still I'm permanently stuck here anyway. I had been trying to find my keys to life ever since I landed on this island. Nothing made sense to me anymore and I was tired of trying to make it so.

*Just have faith.* I could hear my mom saying with crystal clarity. *Be happy with what was given to you.* I miss my parents every day. They were the kindest and most honest people on this earth, and especially to each other. Unfortunately, I didn't inherit a good portion of their traits.

My mother would indulge me by letting me skip school so we could spend the day together. Her ways were full of love and ever tender. My father was also gentle in his manner yet showed tremendous strength at the same time. He taught me the value of hard work and encouraged my independence. I remember in the early mornings before dawn flicking the porch lights *goodbye* as my father drove off to work, and I waited until he signaled his headlights in return. I would go back upstairs to sleep after our goodbye ritual. It was a private message between us that my mother never knew about. I can't recall why I never mentioned it. Of course, my father never told my mother about when he had seen me drive by behind the wheel of my boyfriend's car. I was fourteen at the time.

After the second yawn and my wine glass empty, I decided to head back inside for some much-needed rest and quietly crawled in next to Hank, hoping not to think about the floating woman or her torn tattoo. Every evening when the night came I revisited the horror, each time weighing heavier on my forehead. Restlessly I tossed in the bed for a very long time before my mind let go of the woman in the water and I surrendered to sleep.

~ ψ ~

"Hurry Molly, or you'll be late again." Diesel smoke puffed from the yellow school bus engine that pulled to a stop where my mother and father impatiently waited for me. Dad was out of his uniform and sporting his best Hagar shirt he always wore camping. Mom was in her short sleeve paisley print shirt with matching polyester shorts. "Come on Molly, this is our stop." She took hold of my hand, showing me the way up the bus steps.

"Where are we going?" It didn't make sense, they were both deceased but here they were right in front of my eyes. I was much smaller and younger, maybe in grade school again.

The driver opened the bus door. He also looked familiar. His face was luminous and full of warmth. I followed my parents up the steps. "Welcome home," he smiled. "Looks like good weather ahead, should be a fun trip for all." He closed the door behind me, put the bus in gear, and drove us away. I found a seat on the bus and sat down, peering out the window only to see a misty white vapor.

"Mom, Dad? Where are you?" My parents were no longer on the bus. "Stop the bus, you have to stop now. Wait, they're not here, they didn't make it onto the bus, we have to stop," I hollered at the driver.

"Don't worry, be patient Molly, you'll see them in due time. Of course, only if you pick the right bus stop." He winked.

"Wait, what? What do you mean by that? What are you talking about? My luck doesn't roll that way. I never pick the right stop, or card or lottery ticket." Panic set in then and an onslaught of grief flowed over me. I had lost them both just as before. "I can't do this again, it's too painful," I cried.

"Hush now, you just need a little more faith," the driver spoke to me from the rearview mirror.

"Faith in what?"

"In me silly, I know the way."

"But I don't understand, the way to where?"

"No buts about it Molly, I am the only way to where you want to go. I have repeated these words for thousands of years but you never fully listened. Open your heart and you will know. Have a little faith."

"Just have some faith huh? You make it sound easy. "

"Here give me your hand, I will show you. Come with me." The driver stood up and placed his warm hand on mine and we drifted into the white air.

"Will I see my parents there?"

"When it's time."

"How will I know when it's time? How do I even get there?"

"Don't you understand what I say to you? I am the true and only way. To have faith is to believe in me."

The driver's words draped around me in a peaceful bliss as he drifted away, dissipating into the white.

~ ψ ~

Straining blurry eyes into focus on the cell phone charging on the nightstand next to my head, I picked it up and immediately dialed my parent's house. The irritating screechy tone of a phone that's long been disconnected blared in my ear. I often call their house landline, secretly hoping that maybe they will one day answer my call, maybe someday when my last line is written.

"Are you okay?" Hank sat up, pushing the bed cover back.

"Jesus has a tattoo."

"What are you talking about, Molly?"

"I don't know what's happening to me."

"Come back to bed, it will be alright in the morning." Hank opened his arms and laid me down next to him.

"Can I ask you something?" A lump formed in my throat.

"Shush, go to sleep now."

"Do you ever think about the girl from the water?"

Hank tightened his arms around and buried his face in my neck. "I try not to, but it's hard."

"I know," I breathed in a whisper, crying softly until drifting back into sleep.

## - *Eleven* -

Daylight crept into the bedroom. I opened my eyes only a sliver. It was enough to see everything in the room, giving the impression of status quo. The sharp scent of coffee escaped from the kitchen, wafting up the bedroom stairs, accompanied by a symphony of sputtering noises from brown liquid drips singeing the hot plate.

"Wait," I sprang from the bed. What is he doing home? Something wasn't right with this picture. Hank should be out working the water by now. I hustled downstairs to the kitchen to find him sitting there reading the *Daily Times* newspaper.

"What's wrong? Why aren't you working?"

"I'm spending the day with you, sleepyhead."

"I knew something was wrong."

"I think it's just best I stick around home for today."

"Why?"

"You're wound tight as an over-cranked Timex watch .I think we both could use some downtime, don't you?"

"I'm fine. You don't need to babysit me."

"Yeah, I do. You've been having nightmares, and last night you cried yourself to sleep."

"Sorry about that. It seems like I have a lot weighing on my mind lately, as heavy as a ton of bricks. I can't think straight."

"You have every reason to be upset in light of what we recently witnessed, and you're not alone in feeling this way either. It's a tragic shock to the system for us all; it's troubled everyone in Smithtown and it's the first time in the town's history we ever had to lock our doors. "

"I know what you mean. I don't leave the keys in the van's ignition anymore. I used to feel safe."

"You're safe, hon. It's still the same town. It's still the same people. You just need time to deal with it. I know what I'm talking about. A tragedy like the one you experienced will wreak havoc on your mind and leave you out of kilter. Having delayed reactions are normal. Only time will help you heal, and you can't hurry up the process just because you want it too."

"Yes, you're making sense. Guess I'm just frustrated with feeling this way. And what's really is bothering me is I can't stop thinking about her." This was one of those rare moments when we spoke openly in truth and it was the perfect time to come clean with Hank and tell him about the trip to the morgue, tattoo parlor and breaking into the sheriff department's computer, but my personality doesn't always lend itself to do the honorable thing. Besides, a little mystery in a marriage can go a long way.

"I thought we could take the boat out to the beach for a few hours. There's a nice breeze, it should keep the biting insects at bay. It won't be so hot if we leave soon before the sun is overhead. We could bring the dogs to swim if you like."

"Sounds like a plan, Captain. Maybe it's just what I need." I could see how fun in the sun might be the distraction my brain required to recuperate.

"Eat some breakfast. We'll take off when you're ready."

"Okay then, I'll pack some water and snacks and then meet you down at the wharf. I was thinking about bringing wine, do you think it's too early for that?" I smiled for the first time since I could remember.

"Can you hold off until after lunch?" Hank kissed my head then left for the boat.

I threw several of our favorite go-to junk food and water bottles in a Walmart plastic shopping bag then dressed for the day. Excitement hastened me. I was looking forward to getting away from the house, but mostly getting away from my thoughts.

After rounding up Sara and Bam we walked down to the boat to find Earl Leigh's old truck parked next to Hank's. I love the appearance of that rusted-out vintage vehicle; it matched Earl Leigh's exterior. I opened the van door and the dogs bolted to greet them both. Hank was leaning against the truck in deep discussion with Earl Leigh. Their conversation ceased abruptly when I came within earshot.

"What's up, Earl Leigh?"

"Heard about your troubles so I came down to check and see if you are doing alright."

"Fair to middling you could say." I like to use familiar lingo when speaking to the locals.

"I saw that slimeball roll into Smithtown. He's nothing but a bloated tick out of scratching range on a dog's back. Since he's been around, crab pots seem to magically walk off the boats by themselves and a bronze heron statue mysterious took flight last week from Ms. Ilene's front lawn in Fairview. Must have snatched it under the darkness of night because it's a real busy road and someone surely would have seen him. Then again, he's slipperier than motor oil on a hot road after a summer rain. Lucky SOB only received a misdemeanor charge after he robbed the garden center up in Somerville. Even had his face on the security camera, dumbass. Only Nate can step knee-high in dog shit and still come out clean as a whistle."

"Bam bit him hard on his leg," I proudly announced and Hank shot me a look. Guess I forgot to mention that.

"Ha well, he deserved it." Earl Leigh bent down to pet Bam's head. "Good boy, next time bite him in the ass." Bam returned Earl Leigh's affection with a kiss to his mouth.

"Sorry about that, he's fond of you." Embarrassed, I pulled Bam Bam away.

Hank relieved the bags from my hand and loaded the boat with two chairs, both dogs, and then refueled the tank. It was obvious his thoughts were locked in on Nate Herford. "I used to think he was odd, but harmless. I saved his life a few years back, when I first moved here," Hank said matter-of-fact.

"I didn't know that." Intrigued I wondered what else I didn't know about my husband.

"Yeah, it was blowing a gale with snow flurries, ideal weather for duck hunting, you know. He was out on the small island patch near our place hunting all morning. I heard some shots and went to the front window to see what it was and saw this guy out there franticly waving his arms in the air. Tide had come up and dislodged his boat and the wind took it upriver. I ran the skiff out to him just in time too. Hypothermia was setting in and he was turning an ugly color."

Hank told the story in a nonchalant fashion. Across the ditch b the first bridge there was a white wooden cross hammered deep into the needle rush marsh that proved his point. Duck hunting is conducted during the worst, iciest gales which cause numerous frozen deaths every year. I remember one time Walter saying to Hank that if he had a son who wanted to be a duck hunter, he would hit him in the head with a hammer and start over. I don't think I will ever understand the concept of male humor.

"You should have left him to freeze to death out there." Earl Leigh shook his head in disgust.

"Yeah, maybe I should have." Hank's eyes fell into a heavy stare across the water.

"Are we ready to launch?" I needed to get my husband out of here before his mood grew any darker.

"Alright then, I'll leave you folks to it," declared Earl Leigh as he backed the truck up the gravel road with the muffler exploding in misfires all the way.

Hank turned to me. "Storms are coming later today. We need to get going." He started the boat while I untied the bow. Sara and Bam scanned the deck for the leftover crunchy sun-cooked crab parts to either eat or roll in. Bam takes great pleasure in eating anything foul, from dead crabs to rotten animal carcasses unless he rolls in it first, smearing his fur in the foul glob. Fox urine is high on his list and the hardest to wash off, usually making me late since he has a keen sense of when I have an appointment.

Wind coiled across my face as the boat picked up speed away from the wharf across the water, sailing past the very place where I released the body from the eelgrass. The memory stung deep into my chest. Running away did not change the circumstances and a range of emotions quickly flooded my mind. Hank was right about the storm except it was already here, and building its encroaching gloom on the horizon. I glanced back at my husband. His eyes answered in truth and at that moment, I knew that I would never forget the woman in the water and would never be able to find my way back to normal again.

# -*Twelve* -

A hard rain blew in that evening, rolling through the town of Somerville, knocking down branches from the maple trees. Raindrops fell on rooftops in exploding dots, hammering down onto the houses and disturbing their slumbering dwellers.

Visibility was low, making traveling on roads unsafe and difficult. Since he was short-staffed, Walter was stuck with the night shift duty. Although he would rather be at home shouting answers at the *Jeopardy* TV game show from his comfy recliner, he was out cruising the usual rounds, this time fueled with the purpose of finding the jacked-up blue pickup with black rims. It was twilight and Nate would need to feed his habit soon and be out and about looking for a score. Walter knew drug dependency ruled a junkie's world, making Nate predictable in his routine moves.

He parked the cruiser at an Exxon fuel station on Route Thirteen. From there he would have a clear line of sight on the seedy house across the highway, the one Nate had been known to frequent.

"First things first." He looked up at the sky, contemplating the weather before he dodged raindrops to duck into the dry interior space shared between a convenience store and gas station hoagie shop to order a sandwich to go. After exchanging pleasantries with the night shift attendee, Walter settled back in the cruiser and resumed the stakeout, now munching on a turkey and Swiss sub with a large bag of Old Bay Potato Chips and a Hostess Lemon Pie to finish. Listening to the retro country radio station, he checked the hour between bites, watching for the blue pickup with black rims.

"Should be just about time to reload his habit." Wipers slapped water from the windshield. The rain didn't show any sign of letting up but Walter didn't mind waiting to bag his limit. His years of experience hunting wild game had given him the patience he needed for tonight.

"Ha, just like clockwork. Your ass is mine now," Walt whispered as Nate turned off the highway and pulled into the seedy house, shut off the truck then went inside to satisfy his craving. Walter stayed set on the front door waiting for his hunt to begin. Thirty minutes later, Nate left the house, jumped in his truck, and turned onto the southbound lanes. Walter followed behind for miles with the cruiser's headlights off until the road became desolate before lighting up Nate's truck like a Christmas tree. He drew up alongside, waving Nate to pull over. Walt parked in front, blocking the truck from moving any further. He took his time putting on his official uniform rain gear, stepped out into the rain and removed something from the cruiser's trunk before approaching the truck window. He rapped on the glass, shining the Maglite in Nate's face. The red flashing dome lights whirled overhead as he cranked down the truck window.

"Yeah, what do you want?" asked Nate.

"What do I want?" Water dripped from Walter's hat. He moved the light into position, blinding Nate. A second later, the light was replaced by a shotgun. "What I want is for you to leave. I want you to go away somewhere far enough for me to never have to see your ugly face again. Understand what I'm telling you, Mr. Shit-for-brains?"

"Hey man, that ain't legal, get that thing out of my face."

"This is the last chance I'm giving you to rethink your residence." Walter shoved cold metal into the side of his neck. Sweat beaded up on Nate's forehead.

"Okay, okay, I get it. Put that thing away and I'll leave."

"I'm going to follow you to the Virginia state line to make sure you're gone. Now git before I blow your head off."

Nate's shaky hands rolled up the window, started the jacked up truck, and drove off towards Virginia in damp trousers.

Walter walked back to the cruiser smiling to himself. He pulled the shotgun shells from his pocket and returned the shells into the gun's chamber, nestling the gun inside the trunk of the cruiser.

"What a dumb ass," he laughed, then continued the remainder his night shift in the pouring rain.

# - *Thirteen* -

Before he left for work, Hank had written a mile-long list of chores to keep me busy until he came home, which would be much later than his usual since he had taken time off yesterday to spend with me. The list was his way of keeping me out of trouble. Putting together crab trays, cleaning the gross crab house refrigerator and power-washing the foul crab pots were only a few of the dull duties that awaited me this day. I knew what Hank was trying to achieve here but he knows the banalities of this kind of work are torturous, and it will surely be my undoing. A circus monkey can do this kind of work better than me. The morning was still pleasant and the dogs needed their walk, so the unskilled labor camp duties would have to wait until I came back.

I finished my coffee, washed up the breakfast dishes and dressed for the exciting day that lay ahead. I find island life so exhilarating that some days it's all I can do to keep from sticking my head in the oven.

"Walkies," I hollered for the dogs but only Bam Bam responded in excitement. "Where's Sara Jane?" I looked around the house and found her on the bathroom floor. I called her name again but she didn't move. "Baby Girl, wake up." I shook her side and she popped her head up, blinking her foggy eyes. This is the alarming routine I undergo about every morning now and it scares the poop out of me every time.

"Come on Sara, get up, let's go for a walk. I'm sure we can find something interesting for you." I coaxed her achy body from the linoleum floor and she obliged by shuffling her aging feet to the door. Dog leashes are not required in Smithtown because there isn't anywhere for them to run off too. I wouldn't blame them if they tried. Believe me, if I could run away and escape this island I would.

We walked down the road towards the three bridges, escorted by a swarm of dragonflies as they went on about their business combing the ground for bugs, with the Greenhead fly being their main course.

I prefer to walk in the woods in any season. But the winter is grand, with naked black barked trees that stretch in a rebel yell against the sharp cobalt blue skies despite the cold, standing strong and firm. Winter's color is intensified if you take the time to really look at it, not dead but in living color. In winter the forest is resting, storing up energy for spring's detonation of canopied green hues. The winter woods are also a retreat from the biting bugs.

Glossy ibises flew overhead on their daily homage to one of the larger mainland marshes. They return every evening, flying ten miles back across the sound to nest on Tangier Island. I never understood their journey or why they didn't just stay home to begin with. Hank said it's because they can hunt more food on the mainland and nest on the island without the worry of predators.

Bam had his head stuffed inside a water bush, sniffing for critters, and Sara joined his search. At least they were being entertained. Fiddler crabs retreated into the mud when Bam ambled by, invading their space. I also found something of interest; Earl Leigh was outside dipping crab pots into a bin of pastel green paint. The day was looking brighter for me as well.

"What's shaking, pretty lady? Is this a beautiful morning or what?" he asked without looking up. I can always count on Earl Leigh's flattering prose.

"Can't complain, nobody listens anyway. How about you?"

"Woke up not dead and still able to sit up and take nourishment, so it's a good day." Earl Leigh went on about his business, dipping the wire pots and stacking them alongside the shanty to dry. "You picked a good hour for a walk."

"Yeah, getting one in before it gets too hot." I had the urge to blurt out a hundred questions, firing one after another but thought it was better to take it slow and ease him into conversation first. "Can I ask you something?"

"Sure, what do you want to ask me?"

"Why do you dip those pots in paint? Why not buy the vinyl coated wire pots? The work is already done for you."

Earl Leigh stopped working to ponder my question then sat down on a wooden box. He reached in the back pocket of his high cuffed jeans, pulled out a pint of cheap vodka, and took a swig. "Well," he said, waving the bottle in my direction for a taste. I shook my head, declining the offer. He continued, "You see, that's the way my daddy did it and his daddy before. Figured if it was good enough for them then it is for me as well. New ways aren't always the best way of doing things. Vinyl pots might seem like a good idea at the time but they wear down faster and end up costing more in the long run."

Sara and Bam lay down by his feet. Funny how a dog's judgment of character is always spot on. Most people wouldn't give Earl Leigh the time of day.

"Was Earl Leigh your father's name as well?"

"Well no, actually my mother called me *Early* on account I was born two months before I was to begin my time on this earth. My father didn't like it much and legally changed it to Earl Leigh to appease them both, even though it still sounds the same."

"How long have you lived in these parts?"

"Long enough to know too much, and I know you've come here to see me for more than what you're letting on. Let me guess, you want information on what happened to that woman, don't you?"

"Yeah, I guess so." I was caught red-handed. My cheeks flushed, exposing my transparent questioning.

"Careful what you wish for Molly, it may come true and turn out to be your worst nightmare."

"I already have my fair share of nightmares."

"What is it you want then?" Earl Leigh lifted the pint, gauging the liquid contents inside the bottle. "What exactly do you think you will accomplish by chasing your own tail?"

"I dunno, maybe a cure for this affliction of restlessness. I get consumed by it sometimes and piss people off in the process." I hung my head. Earl Leigh brought the truth to the forefront and I had to face it. I can't change who I am. I know I'm difficult on loved ones and that I can drive anyone near me to the point of insanity. "I don't know why I'm like this. I only know I have to help her."

"I know you do." Earl Leigh spoke evenly with conviction.

"Do you know what's the matter with me then?"

"I know exactly what's wrong with you. It's a wanderlust that commands your soul. Curiosity rules your life and you're on a quest for answers to soothe its desire. You can't help it, its God-given so don't even try wrestling with any other way but your true self. That's the secret to life's happiness."

"I wish Hank understood that about me."

"He does, Molly; I see the way he looks at you. It's pure love and it's a rare possession to own. Hold onto it with all your might."

"You have a sweet way with words, Earl Leigh." I knew he was smarter than he let on but never figured him to be a poetic softy.

"Go on now, my head is swelling. Maybe you should start with your questions while I'm still all sugared up."

"I'm not sure where to begin."

Preparing for my inquisition, Earl Leigh slipped the bottle inside his back pocket and sat up straighter, aligning his concentration.

"I'm ready, just ask whatever your heart desires."

"I believe that guy Nate is tied to the woman in some way."

"Why do you say that?"

"It's the timing of his return."

"Yeah, and a lot of stuff has been stolen when he came back to town. What does that have to do with her murder?"

"He was brought in for questioning about his possible connection to another woman who was missing. Her parents called the police when she didn't come home one night. I had seen photos of Nate with a girl at a party and something struck me odd about her; she's high class, probably from a wealthy family, college girl maybe. I don't understand why she would be at a biker party; it's just not her kind of scene."

"What makes you say that?"

"She wears expensive clothing. Whore attire, but expensive."

"You got something there, kid. Have you talked to anyone about this?" Earl Leigh was genuinely interested and the first person to listen to my concerns.

"I tried telling Walter but he blew me off."

"Why was that?"

"He was mad at me because I sort of broke into his computer and read Nate's rap sheet. I saw the pictures in his file."

"Ha, I bet he was pissed." Earl Leigh snorted several laughs before continuing. "There must be more you're not telling. What else do you know about that weasel?"

"Nothing that would be out of the ordinary except I also saw his photo on the wall in a tattoo parlor in Salisbury."

"Why on earth were you in a tattoo parlor?"

"I was investigating a possible lead. I wanted to find out about a specific design, the one they found on the woman from the water. It was a chunky-looking design of a bird."

"I know what you've been seeking," Earl Leigh's voice lowered.

"Have you seen it then?"

"Yes, I have, many times. It's a symbol of brotherhood that belongs to a certain motorcycle group, the Road Hawks. You don't want to go near that, it's not an upstanding kind of club. Nate's been a member for years, lots of drugs and parties. I believe that was the beginning of the end for him. It certainly was the end for his friend Victor. I heard they have a way of cleaning up any discrepancies amongst themselves."

"Do the police know about this?"

"I'm sure they're very aware of their activities."

"I knew there was something awful about Nate, and it has sat in my craw ever since that day he cornered me in the crab house and startled me, to say the least. He is truly crazy behind those steely eyes." Goosebumps rose on my arms.

"Don't let those eyes fool you. He's skilled in the art of bullshitting. Although he's nuttier than an inbred Schnauzer, he ain't stupid enough to get caught." Earl Leigh hesitated, then said, "There may be more to it, more than what the police know."

"Wait, what? Tell me everything." I was captivated by his words, with each syllable lifting me higher. There was a light at the end of the tunnel, and that light was shining hope.

"I am only telling you this to keep you out of harm's way and from finding out about it on your own. There is more evil in this world than you ever could imagine. Sometimes it's closer than you think. It could be right next door and you wouldn't even know it. You need to have your eyes sharp at all times."

"Thanks for the warning, I will try. Now tell me what else you know."

"Well, it's about Nate and his biker buddies. They've been hanging uptown at Rank's Pool Hall Tavern where Walter has been stopping in for a pint after work in plain clothes. One plus one sometimes equals more than two and if there's anyone that can do the math, it's Walter."

"Aw, you know not! Walt wouldn't be seen dead in that bar. He only drinks beer for medicinal purposes. Unless you think he's at Rank's searching for a lead that would connect the bikers to that woman's murder. Is that why he goes in there?"

"Maybe, maybe not, although the pieces sure seem to be falling into place don't they?"

"Yes they sure do," I mumbled.

Earl Leigh gave my shoulder a shake. My hamster wheel was spinning in full tilt. "Molly, promise me you won't go near them. They're nothing but bad news and that's only the half of it."

That was enough to wake me from my haze. "What's the rest of the info then? Tell me everything you know."

Earl Leigh pulled out his flask again and drained what was left of the gleaming liquid. "You're gonna owe me one of these," he exhaled through a steaming breath before tossing the pint into the burn barrel, the bottle clanking to the bottom.

"Of course, next time I go into town."

"Waste no time then." He raised his eyebrow and I nodded.

"I'll go today, I swear." I finally had currency to barter for information.

"In that case, I'll continue. Nate is very low on the biker totem pole. He's just an errand boy, a peon mule for running drugs. Opioids mostly, bootleg heroin, fentanyl and morphine, all which are highly addictive."

"I'm aware of the state-wide epidemic."

"Yeah, the gang is aware of the addiction as well. There's a big profit in opioids since people easily succumb to its dependency. It's my understanding they also use the drugs to control a stable of young women for their pleasure. A harem, per se."

"That's what I had seen in the photos then, on Walt's computer. It totally makes sense to me now. So, do the authorities know about this?"

"Yes, but again, proving it is something else. It borders on prostitution and sex trafficking. Problem is none of the girls will talk."

"What you are saying is too horrible to fathom. I can't believe they won't do anything about the illegal drugs. The women are kept as drugged-up hostages for cripes' sake."

"They can't and what's worse is the whole operation is conducted in town right under their noses. The florist shop is their front."

"Wait a minute. Do you mean the Sunshine Flower Shop on Main Street next to State Liquors?"

"Yeah, Sunshine Sex Shop would be more like it."

"I've purchased flowers from there several times in the past. It's hard to believe that Mr. Peters could possibly be mixed up in this. It can't be true; he's quiet, a real nerdy dork." The idea of Peters' involvement in abusing women spun my head in circles. Was I hearing this right? "But he seems so mild-mannered, harmless, really."

"He very well may be but letting a bunch of scumbag bikers use his shop for running drugs in exchange for some girly action ain't so nice, now is it?"

"No, I guess not." I was sickened.

"No, it ain't. Drugging women for their sexual pleasures is just plain sick. I heard an official or two are getting a kickback from the operation, and that's a vicious cycle. I also heard that one of them officials fancies a dip in the pool every now and then, and sometimes he swims in the kiddie pool."

"You are kidding me, aren't you? Underage girls?"

"Yepper."

"Who are you talking about?"

"I can't tell you but it starts with an M and ends with AYOR."

"That is horrible."

"Sure is. I hope I'm wrong."

"Good Lord, I thought he was a family man."

"He is, or so it seems in public. I'm sure the wife knows, they always seem to find out."

"Why on earth would she put up with his indiscretions?"

"She comes from big money; it would be a generational embarrassment if the word got out. I believe she turns a blind eye to his affairs because his county position gives them a foothold in the upper echelon clique. All I have to say is he must be a crack conversationalist at dinner parties." Earl Leigh stood up and started rooting through his old truck, checking between the seats and the glove box for a bottle only to find two empty pints. "This afternoon right?" he shook the bottles at me. "Don't want to drive there and end up spending the night in the county drunk tank again."

"Yes, as soon as I get my chores done I'll go into town."

"Alright then, I'll finish telling you what I know. That geek florist guy pays the biker chicks to have sex with him."

"Aw, you know not! That's disgusting."

"It gets worse."

"How can it get worse than everything you just told me?"

"He makes them wear his mother's old clothes."

"I think I'm going to hurl." I held my head still with my hands. "How do you know about this?"

"I can't say how but I can say nobody pays a lick of attention to me so I hear more than I should. What I know for sure is that one of the women he brought back to his house must not have had enough drugs in her system because when he told her about his mommy-dress desires she refused and it sent him into a frenzied manic state. He became irate and started pushing her around. She fought back, calling him a freak of nature, the very same way his old girlfriend did twenty years ago. She humiliated him and his kinkiness."

Any moment now my head was going to pop off and roll across the ground. This was way too much information for me to handle all at once but on the other hand, I had validation from Earl Leigh that I needed to feed on. "I have to go now. Thank you for everything. I'll drop that package off for you on my way back." I jumped up immediately and so did the dogs. We left the shanty without hearing what Earl Leigh was saying.

"Heed my words Molly Hanson, or you will live to regret it. That is, if you're lucky."

## - *Fourteen* -

With a stitch stabbing at my side, I ran home to finish my chores as fast as possible. I folded crab trays, piling them high on the crab house counter. Then I checked the floats for soft crabs and secured the pump, downspouts and the water levels, wiped the disgusting crab house refrigerator down with bleach and hosed off the dried eelgrass from the crab pots. The dishes sitting in the sink since last night's dinner would have to wait until I got back and so would the trash. Although Hank's list was tediously lengthy I still managed to complete everything he requested and expected to be able to return to the island before he did. He didn't even need to know I left home. As I like to say, a little mystery goes a long way in a marriage. Amazing how I can justify my actions.

Rummaging through my closet, I found a stretchy V-neck shirt and form-fitting cropped jeans to wear, and checked myself in the mirror. "Lipstick should do the trick," I said and applied the fire-engine-red waxy color to my lips, achieving the "come hither" look I was after without looking too easy. Still, I wasn't sure if putting the effort into this sort of fashion statement was worth it. I hadn't a clue what I was about to get into, but instinct told me it was best to be prepared for anything from now on.

Sara Jane and Bam were already sleeping on the couch. I petted the tops of their heads, tossed them a cookie and locked the door behind me, which I was still not used to doing. I jumped into the van and just as quickly jumped out of it after landing on the soaked driver's seat from the rainstorm last night.

"Aw, you know not," I said, and went back inside the house for a towel, repeated the dog cookie toss, secured the door, and drove through the marsh, heading for the liquor store and who knows what else.

Surprisingly, the sedate little town of Somerville was hip-hopping today with barely a place to park except over near the courthouse. "Must be a light day on the docket," I wondered, and then remembered my name was on that docket not too long ago for broadsiding a State Trooper in the Walmart parking lot.

The streets were busy with people window-shopping antiques, sprawled out over the shaded square's lawn and strolling through the farmers market. It was a scene from an old black and white movie, so safe and innocent. Little did anyone know what horrors lurked only one block away from the center of the town square. I parked near the courthouse, locked up the van, and walked down the sidewalk towards the State Liquor store, passing by the floral shop. It gave me the willies thinking how I frequented the place; I too was that naïve character in that black and white movie. I noticed a sign on the door. Scribbled in blue ballpoint pen ink were the words *Closed, Re-open tomorrow.* It wasn't just closed for lunch; it was closed for the day and for some reason I found that suspicious.

"What is that pipsqueak pervert up to today?" I cupped my hands around my eyes and peered through the big bay window. It was too dark inside to see past the counter. "Dead as a doornail," I said to no one and continued next door into the liquor store for Earl Leigh's vodka.

The booze distributor was quiet, still early in the day for alcoholic day drinker sales. I didn't notice anyone working behind the counter that ran along the wall, separating the customers from the vast amount of colored bottles on shelves running up to the ceiling, until a raspy voice spoke.

"Can I help you?" inquired an old skinny woman who seemed to suddenly appear. She was petite and not much taller than the counter she stood behind, blending her in with the interior. Her hair was snow white, matching her ironed white blouse. Unfortunately, the years had left the rest of her wrinkled from head to toe.

"Oh, you startled me."

"Yeah, I have that effect on people. So, what do you want? I don't have all day to stand around here waiting." The old woman stared at me in disdain.

"Um, I need some vodka."

"Well, you came to the right place then. What kind do you want?"

"I don't know."

"Boy, you're a real bright bulb."

"No need to be mean. Maybe you can suggest a brand."

"I don't drink alcohol," she snapped.

"Cheap I guess. Give me the cheap stuff." This lady was a real doozie.

"What size?" she groaned.

"I'll take the big one please." I really wanted to say something about her work ethic but held off, knowing she might be useful in obtaining information about the flower shop's seedy operations.

"Here you go, big spender." She handed me half-gallon of Mr. Pops Vodka in a brown bag. "You can strip paint with it as well."

"Thank you," I answered and handed her a twenty dollar bill. She punched numbers into a cash register that could have been created the same year that she was born.

"Can I ask you a question?"

"About what?" she asked, raising her eyebrow.

"How well do you know Mr. Peters?"

"You mean that little wiener next door? I pay him no mind, sticks to himself mostly."

"Where is he?"

She shrugged. "He usually arrives on time every day, except for today." She wasn't the wealth of information I had hoped for.

"Okay, thanks." Strike one. Disappointed, I turned for the door.

"Sometimes there's several motorcycles outback. Don't know what that's about other than a bunch of noise."

I stopped in my tracks when I heard her say that. I was back in the game. "How often do they come?"

"Sometimes twice a day, coming and going. Why, what's it to you?"

"Nothing really, just found it interesting."

"He lives behind the shop, did you know that?"

"No, I didn't know that." Oh yeah, the old bat was toying with me. She was a player.

"You can't see it from the back road. He built a brick wall around the yard and I'll tell you something else about it," she paused knowing she had me hooked, line and sinker to boot.

"What is it?" This cranky woman knew that I wanted to leave here with more than a bottle of vodka in hand, sly old broad.

"It stinks."

"Stinks?"

"Yeah, the whole place smells like vomit. Both the yard and the house have an odor that rolls into the store with the customers on a breeze. They think it comes from me."

"That's strange. What do you think it could be?"

"I bet you dollars to donuts it's something dead and it's decaying in that house."

"I hope you're not right about that. Maybe he doesn't take out his trash often enough."

"No, that ain't it; I know what trash smells like. This is the smell of death, I tell you. I should know, I am close to it." The woman pointed her arthritic boney finger towards me instead of herself.

"I think you're a little spooky."

"And I think your lipstick makes you look like a hooker."

"Okay, you have a point there."

"Yeah, and it's on top of your head."

"Got to run now, thanks for your help." Needing to get as far away from that loon as possible, I stepped out onto the sidewalk, sniffing the air just in case she was right. "Smells okay to me, crazy woman." The once-boring day I had planned for me had shifted into high gear. What the hell was she talking about? There wasn't any odor coming from Peters' house. I went back to the van and started it up. "Time to check in on Walter, let the shenanigans roll," I smiled, and pointed the van for Rank's Bar.

The dreary gray cement building was adorned with intimidating shiny motorcycles and a large sign with stylized letters along a pool stick that boldly announced Rank's *Bar and Pool Hall* over its façade. I squeezed the van in between two Harleys, careful not to bang one with the car door, or worse, knock them over in domino fashion. That would be more like my luck. I looked around the lot and didn't see Walter's personal truck parked anywhere. Was that a good or a bad thing? Walt's conversation suddenly pricked at my memory, replaying like a badly scratched CD with his grim explanation of society. He could have been overreacting, and maybe Peters wasn't so bad after all. I'm not certain paying for his date made him evil. He was a big fat loser after all and they can get lonely, just like everyone else. I supposed that for the girls, it was just a party at first before it all went south and they ended up drugged out of their minds.

I looked hard at the building. "Who am I kidding?" I smacked my forehead. The guy is a creep no matter how you look at it, and probably has some sort of version of psychopath personality disorder just like Walt said. Lord knows I'm not a prize to live with either. Wonder how many categories I fall under.

My attention turned to my poor husband and I again felt sorry for him. I know I don't deserve him. All too often he ends up bearing the brunt of my behavior. I don't know why he puts up with me. In all seriousness, did I really need to be sitting in front of this bar when I should be home cleaning the house or cooking up some food for

Hank, with gravy? Maybe it was time to start questioning my own motives instead of Peters'.

I sat in the van, fixed on the bar's entrance door and batting morality over a net. It's hard to fathom to what extent any one person could be capable of doing under certain circumstances.

"This is ridiculous. Maybe I should come back another time when Walt is here."

My mind buzzed over the edge to the dark side. I knew what I was doing was dangerous and I knew I should leave immediately but true to form, I rejected reason, leaving the van and going inside the bar.

The pool hall was dimly lit by the neon beer signs that hung above the bar. I waited a moment for my eyes to adjust before spying an empty stool. From the back room, voices and the clanking of pool balls floated outward. I sat down on the stool, leaning my arms on the sticky wooden bar. The room held the leftover stench of last night's stale beer. Anxiety coursed through my veins, pulsating in my temples.

"What do ya want?" asked a man behind the bar.

"A draft, please." That was the extent of our conversation. He poured the frothy beverage into a frosted mug then plopped it down in front of me, foam running down the sides.

"Thanks," I nodded and laid a ten on the bar. Looking around the room I noticed that the patrons were comprised mostly of bikers dressed in black leathers, except for a couple of construction workers probably cooling off from the day in the dark air conditioning. I could barely see a couple of women sitting in a corner booth through the darkness.

A dark long-haired fellow at the bar brought cocktails to their table. He was dressed in black leather pants with a black T-shirt and denim vest with various symbols sewn to the material. Other than "Road Hawks" scrawled across the back, I hadn't a clue what the other stuff meant on the vest. He sat down and started kissing the woman's neck, groping her legs. My conscience yanked at my sensible side. It wasn't like I had never been inside a bar before today, just not one as seedy as Rank's.

"What am I doing here?" I whispered, suddenly realizing how obviously out of place I was and motioned to the bartender for my tab. "Six bucks," he grumbled. I pushed the stool in, left the ten dollar bill on the counter for the bartender, and gathered up my sorry butt for home where I belonged, back to the tiny island where all is safe and boring and where I could forget this day ever happened.

That's what I should have done, but destiny has a mind of its own. The corner of my eye was caught by the glistening bald spot beaming through dark brown dyed hair. There he was, short stature sporting a tweed jacket, the same one he wore the last time I visited his flower shop. He was making a beeline in my direction with his black-framed coke-bottle glasses locked in on his target and I was the one in the crosshairs. How did I not notice him in the bar? How long had he been watching me? My stomach twisted as he approached. *No keep going, don't stop.* I positioned the barstools as a barricade.

"Don't I know you?" Peter smiled at his new quest, pinned like a butterfly in a collector's display case.

"No, I don't think you do." *Please go away.*

"Well then I can remedy that," he said leaning in, stroking my arm with the back of his hand. "My name is Frederick Peters, but you can just call me Fritz. Let me buy you a drink, or would you prefer beer? I'm sure I know you. I have seen you before, haven't I?" He beamed with confidence.

"No thank you, I was just leaving." This was beginning to play out like a cheesy summer drive-in movie.

"Aw, why so soon? You and I could have a lot of fun, don't you think? We could go back to my place, it's not far." Peters pushed in between the stools and put his hand on my shoulder. I brushed his hand away.

"No means no, what are you, thick as two short planks?" I stood up, moving towards the pool room. He followed. I was trapped and started to panic. I needed to pull my snappy self together. This is, after all, why I came here.

"But you didn't tell me your name," his pathetic voice whined. "Tell me your name." Peters stood way too close, invading my space for the upper hand.

"None ya."

"None ya?" asked a puzzled Peters.

"None ya business, you moron," I mocked, turning towards the pool tables. Tattooed arms dominated the area. It was a virtual ink art smorgasbord and dizzying to the eyes. I scanned each arm, studying in detail, searching for a sign or anything to help that woman from the water. Some sort of clue just had to be here in the room. I knew it and couldn't give up now. I turned in circles until someone grabbed my arm, startling me to the core. Peters was, if anything, persistent.

"Hey, I was still talking to you," he scorned.

"Let go of my arm you asshole," I yelled, yanking free from his grip and looked around for help from anyone. My eyes locked on a familiar face from the Blue Moon Tattoo parlor, the big biker guy sporting his brand new tat. He had recognized me as well. "What are you doing here?" His voice was deep and hoarse as if he swallowed a handful of gravel stones. He scared me a little.

"I stopped in for a beer." I knew I was close to being in some sort of trouble and tried my best to sound confident.

"You don't belong in here." He loomed overhead. I remember him being tall but had no idea he was the size of Bigfoot.

"Ya think?" This was not the time for snarky tones but I couldn't help it.

"Maybe you should go back to where you came from. This is no place for you."

"Sounds like a smart idea. I was just going anyway." My words fell from my mouth in a stammer. I spun around to flee only to slam face-first into a man's denim vest-covered chest. On his arm was a bird tattoo, and it looked like the very same picture that was on the girl from the water. The air was suddenly sucked from the room. I closed my eyes wishing I had a Batman cape. My heart beat frantically and I thought at any moment I would be meeting the big guy in the sky. I couldn't die this way, not here, not in a bar. That would be too embarrassing for Hank. I opened my eyes to see a pockmarked face. "Where do you think you are going?" he rasped.

"I was just leaving." I had to get out immediately.

"I don't think so," he hummed, sliding his index finger up my throat. "Why don't you stay? We can use a pretty little thing like you. I can make you real comfortable; we're all just one big happy family around here. We live by one rule, one way and that's my way." He sank his nose into my hair, grabbing the back of my neck and pulling me into his vested chest. I pushed against his grip but he cupped my chin with his hand, lifting it towards his mouth.

"Stop it, that's enough," yelled the bartender before realizing the mistake he made.

The pockfaced man released my neck then daggered a stare at the shrinking bartender. "You got a problem? I can take care of it for you."

"No, no it's okay." He retreated, his head down, averting the biker's gaze and mindlessly began wiping the bar's shellacked wood.

The pockmarked man turned his attention back to me, "Hmmm, I'm bored with you now," his murmured voice vibrated against my cheek.

I turned tail and hurried towards the exit. A gathering of amused laughter rose as I ran the gauntlet, knocking over several chairs in my path and out to my van, shoving the keys into the ignition and locking the doors just in case someone was following.

"Wait what am I doing in the van? I'm not going to learn anything sitting here," I said, then got of the van and walked over to the bar window squatting low under the sill and listened.

Inside the bar, the din continued in its normal custom. Pool balls clacked and the beer mugs clinked. Before long, it sounded like an argument broke out over the game with loud words exchanged. There must have been shoving, since I heard tables screeching across the floor. Quietly, I stood slightly peeking in the window and saw the pockfaced man call Peters over and speak into his ear. I would have given anything to hear what was said.

Peters stood back for a moment, then responded with a nod. "Understood," he mouthed, then gathered one of the stoner girls from the corner booth and proceeded to leave the bar.

I ran back to watch them from the safety of my van as Peters loaded the girl like a sack of potatoes tumbling into his florist delivery wagon. It was hard to believe everything Earl Leigh had told me was true. Impossibly surreal, but true. There is a whole big bad dark world out there I was utterly unaware of and it was closer than I had ever imagined. Smithtown is not impervious from its danger. It came down on us like a summer hurricane ripping through the town, lacing its grimy fingers through every resident's core and leaving us naked, exposing our fears and frightening our hearts forever.

Cautiously I started the van and drove down the highway until my heartbeat returned to its normal sinus rhythm. I could never go back to Rank's now, even if Walter was there. In reality, this was a very dangerous game I was playing and I needed to stop the nonsense before I got in any more trouble.

"If only I could stop." I knew I would never find a way out of this. I twisted the volume button on the car radio to full blast, blocking the thoughts whizzing through my head on the drive back home to my ordinary, protected, secluded life in Smithtown where Hank's truck was already parked in the driveway, offloading crabs. Crap, I was caught. But caught doing what? I didn't do anything wrong, sort of.

The dogs were outside and greeted me with happy barks. Smiling, Hank set down a heavy basket of crabs and walked over to nab a kiss. I melted in relief to see his face. How could I have acted so stupid? If I only understood why I am so willing to jeopardize the only thing important to me. This is where I belong. Right then and there I promised myself to never to do anything foolish again. No more dancing in my pajamas barefoot through the snowflakes on a full moon.

Hank drew me close by my waist and kissed me hard. "Wait, do you smell like beer?" he asked, pulling away.

"Maybe."

"Whatever it is Molly, I don't want to know about it or why you weren't home where you belong, taking care of these crabs. Half of the crabs in the floats have hardened up to stone while you were gone doing lord knows what."

"I'm sorry, Hank."

"It's not like you have a lot of responsibility around here. I work my ass off every day."

"I said I'm sorry."

"That's the problem, Molly, you're always sorry. You don't care about anybody or anything other than yourself. And it's getting really old." Hank was fuming and thought it best not to mention being sorry again.

"I had a long hot day and am more tired than a long-tailed cat in a rocking chair factory. I just want to go lay down for a while. We'll talk about this later but for now, I'm weary. Let me rest." Hank finished unloading the crabs, took off his oilskins and hung them on the hook by the back door before going upstairs and shutting the door behind him.

"Not so perfect now are you?" I grumbled at my husband's not-so-shiny superman persona. But he was right. I shouldn't have said that. Sometimes I hate it when the Jersey in me leaks out. My mouth fires faster than I can think. I went to the kitchen and poured my usual glass of self-pity chardonnay and sat there in a huge puddle of embarrassment with my latest buffoonery escapade for company. There are some days when I can land my arrows smack center in the bull's-eye while blindfolded, but on the majority of my days, I miss the mark by a mile.

## - *Fifteen* -

Surprisingly, I woke up with a clear head after the three glasses of wine I downed before falling asleep last night. I actually felt revived with hope and a sense of relief. It was a good day to start over. Yes, a fresh beginning, time to leave the escapades behind me. I'll fix some coffee, make a plan and see how it goes from there. I sat on the edge of the bed, stretched, and let out a slight yawn. "Aw, you know not." Bam had vomited something yellow on Hank's side of the bed, soaking the linens right down to the mattress.

I stripped the bed of its sheets and blankets, tossed them in the washer, then scrubbed the deep goldenrod vile liquid with bleach that reduced it to a lemon chiffon in color. "This is just great," I moaned. Well, at least it wasn't as bad as when he barfed down the floor vent. And it was a good thing Hank had already left for work. Come to think of it, I didn't hear him leave the house. I must have slept more soundly than I thought.

I went to the kitchen to start the coffee brewing. The pot whined with a stubborn hissy fit. Although the morning had a rough start, the day was promising with possibilities. I still had a chance to change my fate.

"Sara, Bam, time to go outside," I called out, and they responded in their expected excitement, bounding for the open door. With coffee in hand, I stepped outside to find a shoebox sitting on the back porch cement steps. "That's strange," I thought, prying off the note attached to the box with tape. It was the size of a business card with a handwritten phrase *Thinking of You*. Cautiously, I removed the lid and was instantly hit by a wave of nauseating air that filled my nostrils down to my lungs.

The strong odor shoved me back on my heels. The box slipped from my hands, crashing to the ground and spilling its contents. The disgusting smell intensified as an odd cactus flower rolled out from its container. Bam gave it a sniff then peed on it. "No, get away from that thing," I shouted and quickly corralled the dogs, securing them inside the house before Bam could roll on the smelly cactus. I kicked the plant back into the shoebox and slammed the lid. Never before had I seen a cactus like that or smelled anything that bad. Why on earth would someone leave this thing on my porch and what the hell was I going to do with it now? Maybe I should go back to bed and try my new life again tomorrow.

"Stop being a weenie," I said to no one, and decided to take it down to the answer man. Besides, in last night's frenzied state I'd forgotten to deliver the vodka bottle and needed to stay in his good graces.

I reached the broken-down crab shanty out of breath and knocked hard on the screen door, presenting the box for his expertise.

"Good Lord Molly, I could smell your arrival before laying my peepers on you." Earl Leigh stepped outside, turning his head away from the offensive odor.

"I know, I'm sorry about that but it's the reason I need your help. And also to give you this." I handed over the liquid remedy and a gooey smile washed over his face as if he was dreaming about puppies.

"I was beginning to believe you had forsaken me." Earl Leigh twisted open the top, said "Come to Papa," and took a big swig from the bottle. I shuddered. He continued, "Now I'm ready to see what you got in that stinky box."

I set the box down on the ground and toed the lid off with my flip flop. "I found this on my steps this morning. I don't know where or who it came from." I stepped back, well out of the odor's range.

"You went to Rank's against my warnings didn't you?" Earl Leigh's demeanor drastically changed. He was no longer the silly storyteller I had come to know.

"How do you know that?" I was surprised by his knowledge of my whereabouts.

"You put yourself in danger by going there. It's my fault for giving you too much information. I thought it would ease your mind, not send you off running towards harm."

"But as you can see, I am just fine as can be, really I am. And believe me when I say I'm never ever going back to that bar again." I was telling the truth, or at least a close resemblance of the truth.

"I would like to believe you, Molly. We are friends after all, yes? And true friends don't lie to each other."

"Yes, true friends. I'm sorry I didn't listen to your concerns. Still friends, then?" I held out my hand to his but he pulled his hand back to his side.

"Wash your hands in vinegar to cut the smell. It'll neutralize it to a dull stench."

"So, I take you have seen, or should I say smelled, this flower before?" I looked at Earl Leigh's eyes. He was trapped in thought from another place in history.

"Oh yeah, once upon a time, back in the day."

"Where on earth did you see it?"

"It was at the Garden Society's summer show. The garden club has a couple of shows a year, snooty show-off shows I called them. I was a member back then, even held second prize for my zinnias." He flipped his head, pointing at the bright orange and pink colored flowers that lined the shanty.

"Yes, I can see that, they are beautiful." Earl Leigh belonged to a garden club. Nothing shocked me about this squirrely haired man.

"Well, this here flower ain't no kind of beautiful." He took another mouthful without taking his eyes off the revolting cactus bloom.

"Why would someone bring that to a show?"

"Only a warped mind would get enjoyment from growing this foul plant. Its name is the Carrion flower, or sometimes Corpse flower because it emits an odor that smells like decaying flesh. It attracts mostly scavenging flies and beetles as its pollinators.

"It's also a very rare flower. They bloom only for two or maybe three days then reappear only after several years of dormant cycles. There's just one fellow around the parts who would probably grow them."

"Who then? Tell me, please?"

"No, I won't put you in jeopardy anymore. Just toss it over the bridge and be done with the stink flower. Heard it said they can bring bad luck." He put the lid back on the box, tore the note from the lid, placed the card in his pocket then handed the box to me. "Stay away from there. Rank's ain't no place for you." He turned and went back inside his shanty and started plucking another mournful tune I didn't recognize on his banjo.

"Thank you again for your help," I hollered at the door. Then I looked at the box and wondered what to do with it now. The last thing I needed was a bad luck albatross hanging around my neck so I ditched the flower over the bridge's aluminum guard rail like he said to, and put the shoebox in his burn barrel. I walked home still wondering who left the gross package on my doorstep as Earl Leigh's dulcet song lyrics faded in the distance.

Michele M. Green

# -Sixteen-

Several times in the past I've heard someone say, "If you don't like your scenery then change it." I had finally come to understand its meaning and decided to get up earlier than usual this morning and make my hardworking husband some breakfast of bacon and eggs with fried potatoes, and gravy on the side just in case. After loading the frying pans with salted butter, I set them on medium heat then turned my attention to coffee making, whisking eggs, and chopping spring onions.

"What the hell is going on in here and why are you up and out of bed at this hour? And dressed as well?" Hank came in through the back door from checking his raccoon traps while waiting for the night to return to day. Each year the crab houses are plagued by raccoons snatching their soft crab bounty from the floats under the cover of darkness. Hank said that when a mother coon teaches her young to hunt from a crab float she only sentences her kin to death. The watermen take no coon prisoners.

I looked down at Hank's feet and raised an eyebrow. He immediately took off his white crab boots and placed them by the door. "Sorry, hon, I forgot. I was put off for a moment and had to make sure I was in the right house."

"Very funny. Sit down, it's about ready."

"So are you actually cooking food or are my eyes playing tricks on me?" Hank said, still skeptical of my actions and my cooking abilities.

"Don't make a big deal out of it. I just wanted to make you something to eat before you head out on the water. When a person works as hard as you do, you need a little substance in your belly." My husband was in total shock. It's not often the house smells of homemade cooked food. I placed a plate on the table, piled high with breakfast, and smiled at him. "You hungry or what?"

"I sure am. It looks great, thank you." Hank hesitated. "So, tell me, what's gotten into you this morning?" He pulled mismatched mugs from the cabinet and poured out two cups of coffee to the brim, spilling slightly over onto the counter.

"Nothing has gotten into me. Just wanted to be nice for a change, is that okay with you?" I said, setting the coffee mugs on the table.

"I was surprised, that's all." Hank sat down and tore into the breakfast spread, savoring every bite. "Boy do I have a story for you. Just came in hot off the CB radio."

I sipped hot coffee in anticipation of his tale. My husband is often contrary in his ways. At times he hasn't a word to say and at other times he will be bursting at the seams with a story, usually embellished with colorful phrasing like *"That man has testicles the size of two peas,"* or *"Those boys ain't got no do-right in them."* Just when I think I have him all figured out, I fall in love with him all over. As for what he sees in me, I have yet to recognize. "Go on. You have my attention now."

"Do you remember meeting a waterman fellow by the name Johnny John at the Kiwanis Oyster Roast last winter?" Hank asked, and I obliged with a nod, though I could neither remember nor be able to tell the difference between Johnny John and any other waterman. All the watermen have silly nicknames like Bunkie, Do Whop or Hung Daddy, and so do their boats unless they're named after their wives. If I had a boat I would name it *The Lady Estrogen* or the *S.S. Va-Jay-Jay* just for spite.

"I heard over in Devils Island early this morning that Johnny had gone off crazy, making a naked spectacle of himself on his crab boat, screaming obscenities at anyone working near enough to hear him."

"What on earth was eating him?"

"He caught his wife kissing on the Deacon at church last Sunday. And that set him on a whirlwind of destruction. Bashed her brand new Ford Focus with a hammer into a heaping pile of metal pulp and then went on to wrecking his house until the police came. It took three head to subdue him this time. They kept him overnight, obviously not long enough because he's out there at it first light. Bet that was some sight to see."

"What do you mean this time? Is there more?"

"Oh yeah there sure is, besides being plumb naked as a baby out on the water, this time it was the Natural Resource and Coast Guard who was called because Johnny swung the boat's patent tongs used for oystering at anyone who came too close and got one hooked on the Coast Guard's boat. That's how Natural Resource Police got on board and I heard it took eight head DNR officers to hold the silly naked bugger down. He'll be spending time in the nut hatch for sure." Finishing his breakfast, Hank chuckled to himself. Johnny's antics may have been speculative rumors but still very vivid.

"Sad what pain a broken heart can cause a person," I commented. The story didn't end as funny as it started.

"Aw, this ain't the first time he's been arrested for acting over the top. It wasn't that long ago a tree branch fell on his shed and dented the metal roof and he went all hari-kari on his neighbor's trees while they were at work. He cut down most of them before the police could get the chain saw away from him."

"If he has a history of craziness, why on earth would you introduce him to me at the Kiwanis Club?" I asked puzzled by his tenuous reasoning.

"He ain't all that bad when he's right in the head," he chuckled.

"Promise you won't invite him to the house, okay?"

"Could be fun."

"Hank, I mean it, keep your distance."

"Hear that wind out there?" Hank moved the subject to neutral.

"Yeah, I hear it."

"Water's gonna be rough this morning."

This made me pensive. "Remember when you told me the wind signals when a change coming? It's just like me I guess. I think a change is coming to me."

Hank put down his fork and grabbed me close from behind, then whispered in my ear, "Just don't go changing too much on me. I don't ever want to lose you, I wouldn't survive that."

The warmth of his voice touched on my neck, burning all the way down my body. "Do you really have to work on the water today? Can't you stay home with me?" I turned, not letting go of his arms. "Maybe you can start a little late this morning?" Despite my pleading I knew he would leave. It was the height of the crabbing season.

"Wish I could," he answered lightly then kissed me long and hard. "I'll try to get back early, we can do something fun then."

"Okay." That was the only response I could come up with.

I finished cooking up what was left of the food as he finished eating from the plate loaded with enough protein to get him through his day. There are very few talents I can lay claim to but I find it astonishing how well I can fake my way through the kitchen.

We finished our breakfast in silence. Hank was preoccupied by the morning news program, keeping a conversation at bay. It was way too early for me to listen to angry voices on television. Politics can really get on my nerves, especially at this hour. I think we would all be better off and much happier if we would just skip all elections or drink alcoholic beverages until it's over. I turned the volume down and tried my best to ignore the noise. "It's nothing but tragic doom and gloom; I don't know how you can stand it."

"It's not all bad."

"Seems like it to me." I didn't have much of an appetite to begin with, and divided up what was left on my plate into the dog's bowls. They gobbled it up so fast I wasn't sure it had a chance to touch their taste buds.

"They don't need leftovers. You're gonna make them fat."

"I know that but I still make extra for them. And they know it."

The wind continued steadily howling against the house. At least it wasn't a gale. "Maybe the winds will let up some after the sun warms the water." I wished he wouldn't go out there in this kind of weather; the last thing I needed was something else to worry about.

"Yeah, maybe it will, I'll be fine either way. Besides, I need to feed my gulls." Hank has a way with animals as much as he does with people and has been feeding a pair of laughing gulls all summer. They land on the cull box, patiently waiting for bunker bait.

"Yes, I hope so." Hank read my expression and got up from the table to give me a hug. "We will continue this later," he purred in my ear and left through the back door without a chance for me to even say goodbye. Guess my turning over a new leaf plan didn't faze him one bit.

I cleaned up the morning dishes, feeling slightly jilted. A commercial about laundry soap blared across the kitchen, insulting my ears, before transitioning seamlessly into the latest local news story with flashing red and blue lights. Yellow caution tape sectioning off the crime scene flapped in the breeze. The television's drone was more annoying than usual this morning. "Damn it Hank, why on earth do you always forget to turn off the idiot box?" I sighed, reaching for the remote. But before I could turn it off, the reporter's tale of woe caught my attention. Proudly standing next to her was a thirty-something man wearing fishing waders and a floppy hat covered with brightly colored fishing lures. They were posed by a bridge on River Road, not far from Smithtown. I thought that possibly someone had driven off the road into the drink again. I try to avoid that road at night because it's densely wooded with a high deer population. The county ran out of street light funding for that area years ago, leaving the area very dark at night and almost impossible to see the road.

I turned the volume up to hear the reporter's words. A photo of a young blonde twenty-something woman mounted the corner of the screen.

*"Authorities have found an item possibly linked to a major investigation of a missing woman. Sandy Morrison was last seen seven weeks ago at Rank's Bar and Pool hall in Somerville, Maryland. Witnesses say she had left alone and was driving her 2012 Silver Ford Escort wearing boot cut jeans, a pink halter top and sandals. Just earlier a break in the case came from a citizen's phone call to the local police department upon discovery of a similar sandal. Sir, can you tell us about what you found?"* The reporter's questioning didn't rattle the fisherman who spoke directly at the cameraman. *"Yes, I returned several times to the sport fishing hole, but never noticed the sandal till I slipped on it and fell on my backside."*

I watched the screen's story unfold as the camera panned to the police who were dusting the shoe for prints and DNA before bagging it, where it would end in the evidence locker. I remembered one time Walter mentioning the procedure to me. He spoke about it at great length. Then it hit me like a sledgehammer to my forehead.

"I know that sandal. It's the same as the one that half-naked girl wore, the one in the photo with Nate. It was on Walt's computer." Blood raced through my veins, pounding in my temples. I couldn't tear away from the TV, as if an invisible force field held me in its gravity beam, tangling my brain with pieces of the evidence. Frozen, I watched the fisherman's lips as he spoke.

*"It was too dark to tell but it was a smaller station wagon type, maybe a Forrester. They didn't see me fishing down on the embankment but I'm certain I saw them dump something in the water then I heard a splash."*

"Bingo! It all makes sense now. Peters drives a Forrester. I saw him leave Rank's in one, greenish-gray in color. It's his floral delivery vehicle." My chest was about to implode. I needed to call someone. Walter was my initial thought, and I picked up my cell, pushing his speed dial number. "No," I said and disconnected. I needed to take my time and think this through first.

The thought of anyone else being harmed overwhelmed my decision-making and I hit redial. No answer. I dialed again listening to the endless ring tone, but no answer. "Third times' a charm," I said and anxiously dialed his number one last time.

"Not now, Molly." Click. The silence was deafening.

I knew Walter's rude manner was my fault. If I phoned him again I could jeopardize any further assistance but I honestly didn't care if I pissed him off. "If you think this will put an end to my pesky pestering," I said to myself, "you got another thing coming your way, butt head." I had just about enough of his cantankerous attitude and immediately dialed again, saying quickly, "Don't hang up." A click echoed in my ear.

"You moron," I screamed at my phone. There was nothing else I could do but sit down and align my thoughts, clear my head for my next move. Ten seconds later I called the sheriff's office landline.

"Somerset County Sheriff's Department," a hurried, out of breath voice answered.

"Did you see the news? That woman's sandal was on TV."

Click. I was beginning to develop a whole new deeper dislike for my husband's friend. My agitation moved swiftly from a simmer to a boil. There was nothing left to do but go to the sheriff's office and come face to face with Walter. But what if he refused to listen to my theory? What would happen to the rest of those women then? Destined for drug dependency and rape for the rest of their lives or possibly murdered?

"No, that's not acceptable. He has to understand." Tears welled up in my eyes. "I have to make him listen," I said, wiping my face. I had to pull myself together. I threw on a T-shirt and a pair of blue jeans then drove as fast as possible until I reached the Somerset County Sheriff's Department where I recognized Walter's squad car in the lot.

"Good, he's at the office, but why at this hour and what's with all the other cop cars?" Several state trooper squad cars and one Somerville police department blue cruiser occupied the small parking lot. Something big was brewing. I parked the van next to Walt's car and tromped up the steps to the front office glass door. It was locked and all of the lobby lights were turned off. I pushed the buzzer and banged on the glass, yelling at the top of my lungs. Walter finally came to the door after a couple of minutes of disruptive door ringing.

"What do you want?" he complained, red-faced.

"It was Nate; he's the one who killed that woman. I saw her sandal on the news, the same one I pointed at in the photo from your computer. She and Nate were both in that picture. He must have something to do with her disappearance." I was almost out of breath. "Open the door and let me in, I need to speak with you."

"Nope."

"But I have more to tell you."

"I heard you were at Rank's bar." Walter's words were tinged with spite.

"Gee whiz, tell me who doesn't know?"

"I bet Hank doesn't," he teased.

"Come on; let me in there will ya?"

"No, Molly, it's official business, I can't let you inside right now." Walter was irritated and didn't seem like he was going to budge.

"Tell me, is that why the building is budding with the Po Po?"

"Go home, I call you later. I've got to go, I'm missing the interrogation."

"Who do you have in there? It's Nate isn't it?"

"Go away and stop badgering me."

"But I have information that may be useful in solving the missing woman's case. It could tie Nate to everything."

"NO."

"Come on, please? You know I'm only going to wear you down until you say yes so you might as well get it over with and open the damn door." I glared hard into his eyes. It gave Walter pause. His skin tone returned to a normal color and his shoulders softened. He inhaled deeply, holding his air before breathing out every last bit of air from his chest. "Are you done?"

"Yes."

"Splendid. "Walter's tone remained level as he unlocked the glass door, shaking his head. Embarrassed by his own judgment he gestured, "Come on," and groaned. Sensing my despair, he opened the door and allowed me to step to inside the lobby.

"Thanks, Walter. I know we don't see eye to eye on anything except Hank but this is important and I think I can help you."

"Look, when we go in there follow my lead. Most importantly, treat me with respect in front of the fellows, you hear me?"

"Of course, but it won't be easy."

"I mean it, Molly." Walt's eyebrow rose.

"Okay I was just teasing, you're so uptight."

"You make me nuts." Walter turned and walked down the hall, speaking in almost a whisper. "We pulled in the delivery boy from the Sunshine Flower Shop for questioning over at the state police barracks but that was nothing but a dead end."

"Did the police find any DNA on the sandal, something that would tie it to her?"

"Unfortunately no, that was disappointing." Walter stopped at one of the smaller offices. "Wait here a minute," he told me, which I did until he came out with a clipboard, a rubber band, reading glasses and clunky black shoes in hand. "Pull your hair back and put these on, you'll look better, more official."

"Whose are these?" I asked, tying my hair back.

"Sherriff Gonzales. Don't worry; I'll put them back when we're through. He'll never know."

I did what he asked, surprised that Gonzales's shoes fit, then tried the readers on. I was a little unsteady walking but my vision was perfect. Though I hate to admit it, I may need to wear glasses.

We continued down the dark hall to the interrogation's one-way mirrored room. Walter put his hand on the knob and said, "Now remember what I said and follow my lead." He opened the door.

"Thanks for assisting us with the investigation, Ms. Hanson," Walt announced, doing his best in not giving me away. The two officers in the room paid no mind to either of us. On the other side of the mirror, four more officers sat at a large gray metal table along with Nate. My heart momentarily came to a halt.

"Like I said, man, my truck was out of gas so I sort of borrowed the Forrester. But I returned it the next morning before dawn when I got some gas for my truck." Nate's forehead beaded with sweat.

"So, that puts you on the bridge the same time as the fisherman stated he had seen the same car you just happened to be driving that evening." The larger officer leaned in close to Nate's face.

"It wasn't me, man. I put it back where I found it. Besides, I have an alibi."

The officer shot a look at the other officers. "This should be interesting," he smirked. "Go on then and tell us where you were."

"I was at Rank's most of the night then went home with one of the hot groupie chicks. We went back to her place over on Fifth and Main Street. She has an apartment over the thrift store; call her and she'll vouch for me. I didn't do anything wrong, just call her. You'll see, she'll say I was there all night long laying on some sweet love." He winked at the mirror and that made me want to hurl on Gonzales's shoes.

"Walt, I need to talk to you," I whispered.

"Not now."

"It's really important."

"I know, but it will have to wait," he waved, dismissing me.

I couldn't just sit here and listen to Nate's disgusting voice one minute longer and I couldn't just sit here when those girls could be in danger. I wasn't wasting any more time. I knew something bad was going to happen; I could feel it in my bones.

Slowly I backed towards the interrogation room's door, sneaking out into the hall. The two officers and Walt didn't notice my departure, not exactly the sharpest knives in the drawer. No wonder they haven't found any leads to the case, big bunch of clueless wonders. I realized then the only person who could help these women was, unfortunately, me.

Despite my nagging conscience's grave warnings I ditched the shoes and glasses, pulled the rubber band with a wad of hair from my head and drove white-knuckled to Rank's bar, sending Morse code signals to the big guy in the sky. "Dear Lord, give me strength."

# -*Seventeen* -

Somehow the bar's mood was different than the last time I stopped in on the joint. Darkness lay over the building as if something sinister had fallen. My inner coward began to kick in and I had to remind myself why I drove to a bar this early in the day. It was because no matter how hard I tried to barricade that floating image from my head she still circled back, haunting to the point of permanent madness. And what pained me the most was that she remained an unidentified murder victim. Somewhere out there someone was still praying for her safe return. I was sitting in front of Rank's bar hoping to bring a sense of closure to her loved ones, maybe a little peace to me, but mostly for that woman who was left in pieces drifting out in the sound.

"This is insane," I whispered. I knew I was standing too close to the edge, but nothing could slow me down or get in my way of helping her, not Walter nor the scary tattooed bikers. For now, I shelved my sensibilities and hoisted my big girl underwear a little higher.

I noticed Peters' Forrester was parked on the side of the lot when I had pulled in. I ran through the facts one last time. The police didn't find any trace of DNA on the sandal, just the fisherman's prints. They had their suspects but lacked concrete evidence: Peters, Nate, tattoos, one preppy sandal, and they still didn't have anything to thread together. My adrenaline ramped up a notch, tossing disconnected dots before my eyes. Maybe I could prod information from Peters, trick him into saying something about the flower shop operations, any little thing that the police were unaware of. I figured it should be easy enough to make Peters spill since he was hot for me or anything that resembled a woman. Depending on how the conversation would go, I'd have one beer, flirt a little and be home in time to put coffee on for Hank. I could do this.

I checked myself in the rearview mirror, wiping the dried toothpaste from the corner of my mouth before moving forward with this crazy idea, although I didn't think it made a difference what I looked like to Peters as long as there's a pulse, and mine was running a marathon. I took a deep breath and reluctantly steered my feet towards the front entrance, stepping into the din of voices where I was greeted by the familiar aroma of leftover stale beer. Scoping the parameters of the room, I realized the scene was far outside my realm of comfort. I suddenly became uncertain about how to proceed with my plan. The bar wasn't as active as the last time; only three bikers were seated in the far red booth, laughing it up. Obviously, their source of merriment stemmed from the six-pack of empty beer bottles that covered the table. The longer-legged man in the booth stood up and hollered out for another round. His deep voice startled me and for a moment my breathing was paralyzed. *You can do this, Molly.*

Pool balls clinked from the back room. I swung my head around to see who it was. Two barely-of-age boys were well into a game. They looked to be local farm boys, probably straight in from the tractor fields, taking a break in the cool dark air. It only took a split second to conclude they were harmless. I relaxed somewhat, pulled a stool up to the wooden bar and ordered a draft beer. The bartender was a step ahead, pouring golden foam into a frosted mug from the tap. He slid the pint down in front of me without a word then went about his business stocking the chest cooler with brown bottles. I was certain he must have remembered my last embarrassing appearance; hopefully, this wouldn't be a repeat performance. I wondered what his story was. Maybe the bartending gig was a second job for him, bringing home a little extra dough. Maybe he too had a loony wife at home, and took the additional job just to get away from her.

I took my time sipping the beer's foamy amber bubbles. It was soothing to my anxious mind and rallied my much-needed courage. I was probably just wasting time sitting at the bar but the beer sure tasted superb. I think it was Benjamin Franklin that said God invented beer to keep man happy. Well, we need more of both in our lives, God and beer. Okay, maybe the beer was going straight to my head. I drained the liquid gold to the last drop then slammed the mug onto the bar just like they do in the cowboy movies. The bartender shot me a look. "Another one?" he speculated.

"Better not," I hesitated but didn't make a move otherwise. After all, I was on a mission and would be a little suspect sitting at the bar without a reason. "Okay, just one more."

"Hello, Molly."

I couldn't see him clearly, just a backlit silhouette from the single window in the bar but there was no mistaking his voice. Peters had his surveillance technique down pat, giving him the upper hand. How long had he been watching me this time? Bizarre, how he could position himself in the manner of an incognito voyeur. Maybe he had the home field advantage but I was ready to kick his balls over the fence.

"How do you know my name?"

"Oh, I remember you from my shop, although it took me a while to place you since we met last, which was, surprisingly, in this bar. I never forget a face, especially one as pretty as yours." Peters slithered nearer and for a moment I believed he hissed at me and I felt my ass cheeks clench. My gut instinct wanted me to haul off and punch him square in the throat, but I had to remain cool and remember my mission. I didn't want to risk impeding his efforts.

"It's not my usual haunt but sometimes a girl needs a little more excitement, if you get my drift." Good thing I squandered countless hours watching vintage black and white movies. At times, I even impress myself with what comes out of my mouth.

"Did you find the little surprise I left for you? That was from my collection. Didn't you find it interesting? I raised those interesting little power plants right at my home and only give them away to someone special, like a woman such as yourself. Attractive, older but still filled in a youthful glow, taller built in a size ten perhaps?" Peters brushed a rogue hair from my face. I stiffened at his touch. Earl Leigh was right. Peters was mentally taking my measurements and it was uncomfortably plain as day I was the same size as his mother. At any moment now the movie *Psycho*'s scary shower scene music was going to blare over the bar's sound system. I wanted to run, but my personal cheerleading squad shouted in my ear, *You can do this.* All I had to do was keep Peters engaged and he would eventually spill.

"Um yes, a little unusual for a gift. I mean, I never had seen anything like that before." I was stumbling. "Thank you, it was thoughtful. Sorry, I did not realize the present was from you." My armpits began to sweat.

"It brings me pleasure to know you can understand great beauty as I do. I find society has lost touch with what really matters, like in that extraordinary rare plant. It will grace us with a bloom only when it feels appreciated, understood for what it truly is." Peters' eyes seemed to have drifted into the back of his head.

"Hello, anybody home?" I was beginning to doubt if any of his brain lights were in working order.

"Oh, yes, please excuse me. I was remembering a time when I was younger. My family has been horticulturists for generations. My mother was particularly talented with her hands, ah yes, she was quite the *Jardinière*. It's a French word, from the feminine form of gardener, you know. Her love for her flowers was as tender as if they were her very own children. I believed she loved them more than her own son. Of course, I was only a silly child at the time."

"The only thing I can manage to grow is mold."

I'd lost Peters' attention. He hadn't heard a single word I said. I swished my hair and stood straighter in an attempt to make my boobs higher to keep him focused on me.

"I have many more varieties at my home and would love to show you. I have cultivated specific plants into a miscellany type of hybrid species. If only Mommy was still with us, she would be so proud of me now. I don't usually allow visitors into my greenhouse but I would gladly show you my little beauties. Oh please say you will come, it's not far, as you already know. I live right behind my flower shop. Please say, yes." Peters was about to burst wide open.

"Sure why not. What have I got to lose?" Like I said, this should be a piece of cake.

"Delightful. I have my car out front, I'll drive us there." Peters clasped his hands and his eyes twinkled.

"Not so fast, mister. Do you have any wine at your house?"

"Unfortunately, no." The twinkle in Peters' eyes instantly faded. "Though I do have a very nice Sherry."

"I'll take my own car and meet you there. I'll bring the wine." Was he nuts thinking I would get in a car with him? But then again, plenty of girls have.

"Excellent, you won't regret this." Peters had a slight drool escape from his lip and could hardly contain himself. I think I actually saw him skip through the door, Lord help me.

By the time I arrived at Peters' shop, his Forrester was already parked on the street. He must have gunned the little car to its limit, breaking the sound barrier. I pulled in behind Peters' wagon, shut the van off and popped in the liquor store next to Sunshine Flowers. I was relieved to see the old woman wasn't running the counter.

"You got this one?" She hollered out from the back stock room.

"Yeah," responded a young man maybe in his late twenties. Thank goodness for him. I couldn't muster up the fortitude needed to deal with the old biddy.

"Can I help you?" he asked.

"Yes thank you, I need two bottles of wine."

He was pleasant enough in helping pick out what I needed to lubricate info from Peters. I paid my bill and gathered up the bottles of chardonnay and merlot I selected, hoping it was enough. I was about to rejoin the short nerdy florist when my cell buzzed. The caller ID read *Hank*. After the fourth ring, I reluctantly picked up. "Hello?"

"Hi, hon. Where are you? I've been home a good hour and a half, thought you would be here by now." A heavy concern strained his voice, and again I was faced with the truth about who I am and what I was about to do, and it wasn't pretty. For the most part, I'm honest, and at times I can be honorable, just not as often as everyone else. Maybe my habitual scheming was a little on the dishonest side but this certainly was for a good cause. The truth would only upset my perfect husband so I did the only thing I could do. I lied. "I'm out shopping at the mall." That was dumb. He knows I hate shopping, especially at the mall. "I won't be much longer, I don't like being here." Nice recovery.

"Okay, I'll go with that. Stay out of trouble and come home soon."

"Will do. Got to go now, love you." I needed to hang up before I said something else stupid.

"Oh, and can you pick up some gravy on your way home?"

"Yes, anything else?"

"Love you too." Satisfied, Hank finished the call, leaving me with serious doubt about my sanity. What was I thinking? Here was a kind, loving, handsome man waiting at home with the coffee ready for me and I was willing to risk all that on a gut feeling. Sometimes I really suck at being a human being.

The florist shop lights were turned off in the storefront, casting an ominous warning that I ignored. I didn't see Peters standing at the glass door but I knew he was waiting for me, and tapped on the pane of glass. A light flicked on from the back of the store. Peters walked up and unlocked the door. "Glad you made it. Do come in, won't you? I was beginning to think you had changed your mind about coming. But that's neither here nor there now. Come, I've made us some tea."

"Tea? But I brought wine." I followed Peters through the shop. The familiar smell of a room full of funeral flowers hung in the air. We went down a long hallway, passing family portraits that hung in gilded ornate frames dating back many years. He stopped, noting one in particular. "This is a photo is of me when I was a small boy." It was a faded black and white portrait of a mother with her young son on her knee. Peters. He wore a bow tie and a pair of knicker trousers. Although she was seated it didn't mask her height. She was tall, like he'd mentioned earlier. And it did not escape my attention that she had a build identical to mine.

"Your mother was very beautiful." Wait, was I feeling some sort of compassion for Peters? Maybe he wasn't so bad after all, just lonely.

"Yes she was, wasn't she? Too bad for me, I take after my father." He led me into a large receiving room filled to the brim with exotic plants, some I had never seen before. Then again, the most exotic place I had ever been was Smithtown.

The high ceilings accommodated two medium-sized cypress trees planted in immense mosaic-tiled containers; one had a red flowering trumpet vine twisting up the trunk. Every nook and cranny oozed a stunning, growing delight. An upright piano, Persian carpets, antique paintings and furniture blended into the background. It truly was a remarkable sight to behold. "This is some jungle you got here, Peters."

"Oh there is more to come." He pointed to another room then opened a door to a spectacular Victorian greenhouse structured with an ornate brass frame. Koi fish swam in a lily pad pond housed in the center. If I didn't know better I would have thought I was in an enchanted garden theme from Disneyland.

"Ah, here it is, this is what I wanted to show you." Peters' center of attention turned towards the other side of the greenhouse. Growing in partitioned groupings were grossly massive but sweetly fragrant flowers. I mistakenly thought them to be yellow daisies, but when I approached they appeared not to be flowers but more of the cactus variety, resembling something from a science fiction movie I had seen in grade school, *Attack of the Killer Daises.*

"Look over there, do you see them? Aren't they fantastic?" Peters boasted. "I'm rather fond of these more than most."

"Yes, they are amazing, striking actually. And their perfume is heavenly." Everything I said was true, but I still sensed something was off. Were the plants intoxicating or did I still have a beer buzz? Or was it that his exuberance was infectious? Either way, I needed to stay on task. "Is there someplace we can sit and talk? We can have some of the wine I brought."

"Oh, where are my manners? Please let me take those to the kitchen. Wine sounds like a splendid idea, but why don't we have tea beforehand? It will prove beneficial when mixing beer and wine. I'll be only a moment. Why don't you make yourself comfortable in the parlor?"

I did what Peters suggested and waited in a paisley-printed wingback chair. Mixed feelings had left me unsettled. I didn't care for his way of schmoozing me off guard. I would rather be having a big glass of wine instead of tea, but I had to placate the dork, for now, to accomplish what I came for. Besides, anymore alcohol in my system and I might be the one spilling the beans. Or worse, start singing Karaoke.

Peters was occupied preparing tea and that left me enough time to snoop around. After sizing up the room's furnishings it was easy to surmise there was probably still a good bit of that old family funding left in the bank. On the end table next to the wingback chair sat a brown leather-bound photo album. I flipped through the dark leaflet pages with shredded edging filled with black and white Polaroids of his mother, each fastened to the page by small black triangles on each corner. The photos spanned across years of her life, dating back to the early fifties. She was very beautiful in stature, tall and lanky thin with blondish hair. Striking to the eyes. It was plain, even obvious now, how similar we were, although she was a little more physically endowed than I am. I'm not sure which is flatter, my ass or my chest. In fact, if you turned me upside down you wouldn't notice whether I was coming or going.

I continued my probing through a mahogany roll top desk and in the middle drawer I found a Polaroid camera and another album, and of course, I opened it. "What the? "I sure wasn't expecting this." Oh, Peters you are one sick bastard." I shook my head at the Polaroid photos lining the pages, only this time they were in color and none of them were of his mother but of young women dressed in his mother's clothing. Towards the back of the album was a bookmark where the pages took on a whole different theme. I suddenly realized that gardening was not his only hobby and that Peters was the one who had taken all the pictures of Nate I saw on Walt's computer, as well as the pictures of naked girls under the command of the motorcycle gang, the Road Hawks. I flipped to the last page. "Aw, you know not." I couldn't believe it with my own eyes. It was a picture of the Mayor, just like Earl Leigh had told me.

The tea kettle's whistle blew, announcing that Peters would return soon. The picture album slipped from my startled hands to the floor and I kicked it out of sight under the wingback chair.

"Ah, here we are. Steamy hot and juicy, just the way mom liked it." Peters balanced a small white china teapot with two matching teacups and saucers on a gold tray engraved with a deer hunting scene. "The set belonged to my great grandmother. See? It bears our family crest." Peters held the scalding pot toward my face.

"Yes I see, in 3-D to be exact," I moved the tray away.

"I hope you like the tea. It's a mixed blend I ordered online directly from India. It's a little pricey but I was taught at a very young age never to scrimp on tea." He smiled and poured the hot black beverage into the cups without taking his eyes off mine.

"You may find the taste a little pungent at first but you will grow to like it, I promise." He handed me the teacup then lifted his cup to his thin lips. "Drink up, it's quite the experience."

I sipped the tea, holding back a gag. A strange aroma rose within the steam. "Yes, it is different as you said. Why don't we open a bottle instead? You can tell me more about yourself, like what else you do for fun besides grow flowers." I was beginning to believe he had brewed the awful tea from the stinky death flower. I needed to hang in there long enough for him to slip up.

"Oh just try a little more, dear. You'll agree it gets much better. I find it very relaxing and you will too."

"Alright, just one more taste." Peters was right, the second sip was smoother and fragrant on my tongue. "This could actually be tastier than wine." Slowly it warmed my mouth, moving down my throat, loosening the words I spoke. "What kind of tea did you say this is?" Why did I sound so drunk? I didn't drink that much at the bar. My arms felt like they were floating on two red balloons tied to my fingers. Why is he still talking? Can't he hear me?

"Here, drink a little more. You will feel much better." Peters held the cup up to my chin then poured a small amount of tea in my mouth as I involuntarily swallowed. "I knew you would be a stubborn little thing but you'll quickly come to understand and enjoy everything I do for you, just as mother did. It's such a shame she passed so suddenly. You would have loved her so. But everyone dies, don't they?" Peters' eyes glazed into a different time zone then whispered "Mommy." He jumped to his feet, clasping his hands together. "It's uncanny how much you two are alike. Oh, this is going to be so much fun, you will see. We are going to be so happy again, just like it used to be." He left the room and went back to where he had made the tea. My thoughts spun wildly. I couldn't move or make a sound. My body was heavy, held captive sinking deep within the chair. What was happening? *Oh God please help me.* I heard rustling from the other room then footsteps coming closer as Peters returned through the door, the bright light filtering from behind him going dark. He came towards me with his arms full; I couldn't make out what he was holding before he placed it on a chair. "Here we go. I think you will be very pleased with these. It's almost party time, I hope you are ready," he said in a monotone scripted voice. He picked up my limp arm then let go. It landed with a heavy thump to my side. "Perfect." He laughed repeatedly, growing louder. I tried to get up and run but no longer had feeling in my legs. Tears ran down my face but I couldn't feel them either. "Hank, help me! "I shouted but couldn't hear my own words, only the wretched sound of Peters' laughter as my eyesight melted into a murky darkness.

~ ψ ~

Earl Leigh was parked curbside across the street from State Liquors. He desperately needed to replenish his daily constitutional supply but remained in the vintage rusted-out truck a long while, trying to recover his bearings before attempting to walk across the street. He sat there long enough to watch Peters come home and go inside by way of the flower shop storefront. "You little weasel. I know you're up to no good, probably with that biker trash. Yeppers, right in the thick of it I bet, doing who knows with who knows tonight," he snarled.

"Wait, what the hell? You have got to be kidding me. What are you up to now, Molly?" Earl Leigh didn't have to wait long for his nerves to sober up after spotting my exit from the liquor store. "No, get away from there. Don't do it." Watching my disappearance into the flower shop was more than enough to completely clear his thoughts. He stumbled from the truck and raced across the street, bursting through the State Liquor's door.

"Let me guess, the unusual for you?" The grouchy woman routinely reached for the larger bottle of vodka without looking.

"No, no I need a phone book and make it snappy. I don't have time for your quips now," Earl Leigh was gasping, out of breath from the jaunt.

"I don't care for your tone," stated the little woman, defiantly placing her hands on her boney hips.

Earl Leigh knew he had met his match and came up with a different approach. "I am so sorry; I lost my head and my manners, but only for a brief moment. I was taken by your beauty. You can understand. I'm sure you have that effect on many men."

"Yes, I do," her shoulders softened. "How can I help you?"

"You see, my friend is in jeopardy and I need to call the sheriff's department but I don't know the number."

"Well, you should have said that in the first place. I have an old phone directory in the office. Wait here." The grumpy woman returned with the thick yellow book and thumped it down on the counter. Dust flew everywhere. "The number should be in there." She flicked through the worn pages, "Yes, here it is," she said then handed the book over to Earl Leigh.

"Thank you so much. Can I bother you for a phone as well?" he crooned.

"Seriously?" she huffed, then pulled out the store's landline phone from under the countertop. "I'll leave you to it then," she said, and returned to the back room.

Earl Leigh had trouble dialing the number, his hands were shaky, either from the lack of alcohol in his system or the fact that I was in the depths of Peters' house.

"Sheriff's Department," answered Walter.

"Thank goodness it's you, Walt. I think Molly is in danger."

"So what else is new?" Walter snorted. "Who is this by the way?"

"It's Earl Leigh from Smithtown."

"I see. Hitting the sauce a little early today, don't ya think?"

"That's incorrect and none of your business."

"Okay then, tell me about Molly. What has she done now?"

"I saw her go into the booze house and come out with a couple bottles of wine."

"So?" Walter held his posture.

"Then she took the wine into Peters' house and never came back out. There is something screwy about that guy. Always has been since I can remember," Earl Leigh shouted. He was completely sober at this point and didn't like it very much.

"And how did you happen to come by and see this all take place?"

"I was waiting across from Sate Liquors."

"Waiting for what?"

"I was waiting because I was well under the influence, too drunk to drive and didn't want to risk breaking the law, officer, being a registered voting upstanding citizen and all."

"You're driving now, ain't ya?"

"Never mind that and listen to what I'm telling you."

Walter did an audible head slap and sighed. "Okay, let it rip."

Earl Leigh took a deep breath. "That Peters fellow cultivated exotic flowers and was a member of the garden club back in the 70's. He was a real looker then but never married because he was a mamma's boy. He doted on her hand and foot vying for her praise, which she never gave because he never could quite measure up to any of her expectations. He lived with her until she died and wouldn't let the undertaker put her in the ground for weeks. Visited the funeral home every day and sat with her for hours, just talking."

"So what does this have to do with anything?" Walter let out a small yawn.

"Open your ears, man. What I am about to tell you has a lot to do with inappropriate doings at Rank's."

"Go on. "Walter sounded like he must have sat up and pressed the phone to his ear.

"Thought that tidbit might grab your attention by the short hairs. Glad you're finally listening. By the way, it's rather rude not to. As I was saying, Peters is a regular at the bar and involved with that unseemly batch of bikers. They are the kind that gives bikers a bad name."

"I am aware of that but not sure what this has to do with Molly being in some sort of peril, unless you mean after I tell her husband about where she is."

"Damn it, man, will you let me finish? Now, where was I? Oh yeah. There was this woman Peters dated for a while. She was pretty, mind you. So was I back in the day. The one thing that stands out is the gal didn't get on with his mother very well. They bickered often and it was terribly hard on Peters, causing tension in their relationship. He wanted to marry the girl, had a ring and all, and even proposed one night at Italian Joe's restaurant over a plate of meatballs. Problem was he wouldn't leave his mother's house, not ever. The evening ended badly in a big public scene. She called him names, humiliated him in front of everyone. She eventually started running around and bedding every guy she could, making damn sure he knew about it. Sure it was all free love, peace and bell bottom jeans back then but she was out of control, flaunting her behavior in broad daylight. She had no shame. No shame at all. Then, just like that, she was suddenly gone without a trace, never to be seen or heard from again. See, Peters' mild-mannered shopkeeper image just don't add up.

"Why didn't you tell me all of this before?"

"Because you never asked me."

"Just sit tight. I'll be there in three minutes."

~ ψ ~

I woke suddenly. Something was pulling on my legs, jerking my body. *Stop it. What are you doing?* It was Peters, roughly yanking pantyhose up my legs and then shoving shoes onto my feet, securing them in place with a button strap that snapped shut. *Why am I on the floor? Don't touch me. Oh, my head.* I screamed but no sound came out of my mouth. Panic gripped my heart. I searched the room and could see my clothes folded neatly in a pile on the green paisley-print wingback chair. *What am I wearing? Wait, stop it, what are you doing?*

"There we are, just like old times, Mother." Peters lifted my body up on the chair, positioning my legs crossed. He stroked my cheek. "Remember how we had fun? Oh Mommy, it's so good to have you home again."

*You freak, don't touch me. Help, help please God don't leave me here.*

I tried to push Peters away but my arms would not move. I tried screaming repeatedly but it fell on deaf ears, for no one could hear my cries.

~ ψ ~

The squad car's siren pierced Earl Leigh's ears, jolting him from a nap in the front seat. "Boy you sure know how to make a grand entrance," he griped as he slowly got out from the truck.

"Come on. I have a complaint from Peters' neighbor about a sickening smell coming from the house. It lured a load of turkey vultures to permanently perch here and I've ignored the complaint for quite some time. It will take too long to get a search warrant but it sure is a good excuse to go poking. We can cut through the alley to the backside on West Street and then go check out the house from behind." Walter took off down the alley with an apprehensive Earl Leigh taking up the rear.

They reached the back yard and peered through the ivy-covered iron-gate, surveying the grounds. Sure enough, seven turkey vultures sat drying their wings on the roof's peak.

"Let's go," said Earl Leigh.

"I can't go any further without a warrant," he said suggestively. "It would be breaking and entering."

"Not if it's open." Earl Leigh pulled a small metal item from his key chain and picked the lock. "Nothing to it," he smiled, and stepped through the gate as the vultures squawked. "Well, I guess the neighbor had a legitimate beef. Kinda creepy, ain't it?"

"Yeah, the whole yard is spooky. The place is in dire need of a serious pruning." The overgrown backyard was covered in exotic plants, bushes and flowering trees. Closer to the house stood a greenhouse with whitewashed windows. Walter walked through the tall grass to have a look through the window. Earl Leigh purposely lagged behind. "I just know I'm gonna be full of chiggers by the time we are through. Maybe get bit by a snake or poisonous spider. Who knows what that whack job considers a pet? Man, this place is a jungle. You don't have a machete by any chance, do you?"

"Come on, will ya? Stop messing about. I just want to have a look around. You can leave if you like." Walter pressed his face against the glass. "I can't see anything."

"It smells bad and getting worse by the minute." Earl Leigh held his arm up, covering his nose and mouth.

"Like I said, that's why the vultures are hanging around. Most likely something died out here and Peters never removed it from the yard. The methane gas revved up from the sun's heat." Walter moved a rotten section of plywood away from the greenhouse, a mouse scurried out, followed by a parade of insects.

"Well, that looks comforting."

"Come on, the greenhouse door is ajar, let's have a peek inside." Walter jiggled the knob and opened the door. The odor hit them like a ton of bricks to the face. "Ugh, that's really bad, step back and cover your nose."

"This is crazy, I ain't going in there with you." Earl Leigh turned his back.

"It's okay, it's just some cactus plants in ceramic pots." Walter cautiously moved inside the greenhouse. Hand-built wooden tables lined the sides of the greenhouse with rows of potted stinky cactus plants on tabletops. House flies swarmed the pots, buzzing in reeking ecstasy.

Earl Leigh poked his head inside. "It's called the Death Flower because it smells like rotten flesh."

"That explains the vultures and the flies." Walter ran his foot over loose dirt under the workbench, exposing decomposing human skin. "But it doesn't explain this," he shouted.

"Man, is that a hand?" Earl Leigh froze in place, wishing he brought his flask along.

Walter was quick and ready on the portable police radio, asking for back up. "10-35 major crime alert, homicide 10-100 dead body found with a possible 10-31 in progress. All units respond to West Street, Somerville, backside of Sunshine Flower Shop. Suspect is present."

"Oh man, this is bad. Let's get out of here."

"Calm down, back up will be here in a minute."

"No way. I don't need to be part of any of this mess. And I don't need to be getting all buddy-buddy with the Po Po. The less I know, the better. Later, man." Earl Leigh turned back, ambling his way through the grass.

"Wait, do you hear that? I can hear music coming from the house, and screaming laughter. It's Peters. Come on, we're going in." Walter held his hand over his gun, leaping out of breath over the garden overgrowth. "Hurry, Molly is in there and if that creep touches her I swear I put a slug in him."

"Only after I get my hands on him," hollered Earl Leigh, pushing ahead of Walter.

~ ψ ~

"Dance with me, Molly, they're playing our song. Isn't this just grand?" Peters waltzed around the room, my head painfully bobbing on my lifeless body. *Oh my God, what did you do to me? Stop jerking me around, you're hurting me.* The music swelled and so did his squealing laughter. Peters' steps swirled by the gold mirror. I caught sight of what I was wearing. A cotton dress with the back unzipped flapped from my shoulder. My arms dangled weightless like a rag doll's. *Whose clothes are these? No, no, stop. Why can't anyone hear me?*

"Oh Mommy, I could dance all night, couldn't you? I have plenty of tea left in the pot." Peters spun my body in circles, screaming over and over. *Please stop I'm so dizzy.* I knew my strength was dwindling. I could feel it draining from my floating body. I couldn't breathe.

"Isn't this just divine? And no one will ever have to know. Go ahead and scream, oh but you can't, can you? Nobody can hear you anyway." Endless sickening laughter controlled Peters' every move.

*Oh God, help me. Please. Hear me, precious Jesus, take my hand.*

~ ψ ~

The tangled grass grabbed at their feet, as they sprinted towards the rear of the house proper. Earl Leigh fell onto the landing, knocking a metal trash bin over.

"Be quiet will ya?" Walter scolded, out of breath. None of this was actually in his wheelhouse.

"Sorry man. What was that doing there?"

"Keep your voice down."

"Why are you whispering? Hell, ain't no one gonna hear us. With all that racket going on in there, I doubt you'd even hear a dump truck driving through a nitroglycerin plant."

"Alright already, let's go inside and find out where it's coming from." Walter opened the screen door finding the interior door unlocked. "Come on," he motioned. Earl

Leigh carefully tagged behind. Their guarded footsteps snaked through the house, suspect of what was lurking behind every closed door they passed, and as the music continued to grow louder so did their fear. Walter held his Maglite shoulder high, his other hand hovering over the holstered gun at his side while Earl Leigh's hands hovered over his gonads. "Place sure has a lot of rooms. A person could hide anywhere and never be heard from again. It's kinda spooky, like the yard. Inside and out."

"Yeah it sure is," Walter mumbled, not paying attention to Earl Leigh's chatter. He stopped and opened a door to the left, shinning the Maglite over antique furniture, built-in bookcases and several plants. "Reading room," he said and continued to another door, carefully pushing it open. "More of the same."

Down the hall, Peters' laughter escalated into maniacal screams.

"Come on man. I went dry and changed my mind. Can we please get out of here?"

"Stop your complaining, will ya?" Walter ignored his grumblings and opened the second to last door. "Whoa cowboy, what's this?" The Maglite's beam played above an old fashioned, white enameled medical table on black castors. The light spanned upward across the whitewashed medical cabinets. Neatly arranged surgical supplies of bandages, medicines and various chrome cutting tools were housed behind the glass.

"That don't look normal to me," Earl Leigh stammered.

"Aw, it's nothing. Back in the day people had a medicinal room set aside, took care of their own doctoring. Did some minor surgery as well, stitches and whatnot." Walter turned around, redirecting his Maglite towards the shrieking behind the last door. "This way."

"I don't like it here. Or that nut bag Peters. Let's go get her out of here before the cops come. I don't like them much either." Earl Leigh's nerve endings were on fire with the jitters, either from the situation Walter had cornered him into or the fact that he was running on empty.

"Not until I know Molly is safe."

"She can probably handle herself."

"Come on keep moving, the sound is coming from in there." Walter gestured towards a swinging restaurant type door. "Must be the kitchen." Earl Leigh was struck with fear, feet glued to the floorboards, staring at the light filtering through the door jam. Walter moved first, peeking one eye through the crack then glanced back over his shoulder. "I have a feeling I'm gonna miss *Jeopardy* again tonight."

"Never mind that, what are we gonna do now? Molly's in there and he's doing who knows what with her. Just shoot the bastard and get it over with. Give me your gun if you ain't gonna do nothing."

Beads of sweat formed over Walter's temples. "We need a plan." His mind clicked into commando mode. His thoughts narrowed smooth and directed, his heart banged in his chest and his blood pressure rose to a thump behind his ears. Walter released his black nine millimeter from its side holster, tightening his grip on the handle and calculating his next move. "On my count, we both shout *Police* and rush him. If he doesn't let her go, I'll pop one off in his leg to bring him down."

"But what about Molly? What if you shoot her by mistake?"

"She'll get over it."

"Why don't we wait for backup?"

"You don't hear no sirens, do you?"

"No."

"What, are you afraid?"

"Yeah, I'm afraid you may shoot me instead."

"You'll get over it."

"Good Lord, you're a cold man."

Walter knew Earl Leigh was right about waiting for backup; after all, it was protocol. But Earl Leigh hadn't looked through the swinging door to see what Peters was doing to Molly, and time was of the essence. Problem was, Walter never had to use a gun for anything other than hunting, and that made his gut ache and his hands shake.

"Oh man, I don't like this at all. This is giving the heebie-jeebies." Earl Leigh's instincts were pulling him as far away as possible.

Walter stretched out his raised gun arm. "Ready? It's now or never."

"I guess so."

"On the count of three. One, two, three." Walter kicked the door, slamming it hard against the wall. "Police, stand down," he shouted as he rushed through the door with an apprehensive Earl Leigh behind him.

~ ψ ~

Peters ignored their shouts. In a trance, he danced, spinning his rag doll faster and faster in circles, singing louder with each twirl as if they were not even there. Around the room we went, over and over like a carnival ride with macabre pipe organ music that could terrorize children. *I have to stop him. Creepy pervert will never do this to women ever again. I'm not afraid of you, you rat bastard.*

With each round, my eyes locked on a vintage wall-mounted pink princess phone. *You can do this. Just move your arm. Yes, that's it, move now!*

Walt held his gun on target, in and out of Peters' swirling legs.

"Shoot him," Earl Leigh shouted.

"I can't get a clear shot." Walter flipped the gun's safety over, steadied his shaky aim then closed one eye and fired as Peters whizzed by the phone.

With an open hand I grabbed at my only hope of escape and tried to smash the receiver into his face, tangling Peters' steps in the long phone cord instead and sending us both tumbling to the floor.

An ear-piercing gunshot shattered the room, rebounding off the walls, and was soon replaced by whimpering cries. Walter opened both eyes to see Earl Leigh with his foot holding down Peters' head. "Did I hit him in the leg?" Walter asked.

"Well no, not exactly in the leg," Earl Leigh grinned, glancing down at Peters. "More like the tail feathers."

Walter slapped a pair of cuffs on Peters then turned his gaze towards a pile of limbs. "Molly!" he gasped and fell, kneeling by my side. I was lying on my face. He turned me over onto my back and straightened my arms and legs. "Molly, can you hear me?" he asked, and laid his face on my chest checking for any sign of life.

"Is she alright?"

"I dunno." Walter immediately called the situation in. "Shots fired, suspect down. Ambulance needed, hurry!"

"Can't you do something, man? Don't let her die, not here, not like that." Earl Leigh clamped heavily on Peters' squirming head with great enjoyment. "Stay still, will ya, you little vermin."

"Why did you stop us? We were only having some fun." Peters bawled. "I'm in pain, help me."

"Help you? You're kidding me, right? It's lousy creeps like you that make this world a fearsome place. I hope they put you away for a long, long time. Little pipsqueaks like you will make a real nice girlfriend for some inmate. Oh yeah, you'll be somebody's little love machine every night."

Peters' wailing increased about a degree more than his laughter. "You can't leave me here like this, I need help. You have to help me, I'm wounded. I might bleed to death."

"Hope springs eternal, you little piece of turd."

"Here, this will shut him up." Walter tossed his stun gun to Earl Leigh.

"Seriously?"

"Knock your socks off."

"With pleasure," Earl Leigh said, then eagerly set the stun gun to high and pushed the button. Peters' body surged with electric shock waves, writhing in agony until he pissed himself and passed out.

"That should do it."

"You need to press your hand on Peters' wound," Walter advised.

"No way man, I ain't touching his ass. Let him bleed out for all I care."

"Okay, okay just use something heavy."

Earl Leigh looked around and spotted a large fern in a terracotta planter and placed it on top of Peters' bloody gunshot wound then joined Walter in kneeling by me. "She's dead, isn't she?"

"No look." Walter wiped a tear from my cheek. "The deceased can't cry. They can fart but they can't make tears."

"Wait, she farted?"

"No you dope, I'm just saying."

"But she ain't moving, like she's dead."

"I don't know what's wrong; he's done something to her. I called for an ambulance, should be here any minute. Yes, I can hear them now."

Police sirens from the distance approached the town block, roaring up the street and blocking sight of the house. Blue and red lights speckled the interior. "In here, we're in here," Walter hollered, then focused on my puddled form. "Can you hear me? Say something please."

I thought I said something, a word or maybe two but nothing that could be heard. *Try again. You got this. Just try harder.* "Photos," my mouth slurred in a drunken state.

"What? What did you say? I can't understand you," Walter couldn't make out my drug-hazed language.

Earl Leigh cupped my lifeless hand in his. "It's going to be alright now darling, and you're safe now," he whispered before making himself scarce.

The ambulance crew burst into the room and instantly crowded around me. Walter was pushed back, lost in their flurry.

"Stop, wait." And there it was, my voice was heard.

"What is it, Molly?" Walter shoved an EMT out of his way, flopping down on his knees.

"The photo album, it's all there. Everything you need is in the album, don't leave without it." Words floated from my lungs as I exhaled.

"Step aside sir, let us work now." The first EMT resumed taking vitals and strapped my body to a board while the other rolled a gurney through the room.

"The album," I said again.

"I will." Walter scrutinized the room, inspecting every inch until his eyes landed on the photo album tucked under the paisley-print wingback chair.

~ ψ ~

Walter was left to wait outside, standing numbly in the street by the ambulance, running over every move in his head, worried if he had handled the procedure by the book. Probably not. This time it was hard to separate his emotions from the job. He was intimate with the victim; she was his best friend's wife, a man who was frantically driving to the hospital right then. He hung his head in doubt as dread commanded his thoughts.

Walt looked on as emergency uniformed men loaded the gurney into the ambulance; a somber appearance claimed their faces.

"I hope that hospital can fix her up," Earl Leigh said. His sudden re-appearance startled Walter.

"Where did you get off to anyway?"

"I believe I may have told you that I have a slight aversion to authorities and figured it was time to git while the getting was good."

Walter sensed the ordeal had taken quite a toll on Earl Leigh. In fact, they were both in shock. He noticed the Somerville Police were occupied tying yellow caution tape across the flower shop crime scene. "Looks like everything is starting to wind down, the detectives will be busy for a while. They can finish up here without us. I think it's alright for you to go home now." Walter held out his right hand. "Thanks for your help, I mean it."

"Anything for Molly. Hey, what time is it getting to be?" Earl Leigh's eyes spanned the storefronts until his thirsty eyes spotted the neon sign that said *Open for Business*. "Great, my favorite haunt is still open and it's calling my name. Maybe the old bat is in a better mood. I could get lucky tonight." Earl Leigh raised his eyebrow and made a beeline for State Liquors. "See you around sheriff," he shouted, and launched across the street with a renewed hitch in his giddy up.

Walter closed the ambulance door and gave a double whack on the rearview window glass. After the day he had, Walter thought about following Earl Leigh's lead but decided to head back to the office to start the paperwork and make that dreaded phone call to a very worried Hank and explain in detail what his wife was up too.

It wouldn't be the first time Walter had to make that troubling call to my husband about me, and the way my luck rolls, it won't be the last.

# - *Eighteen* -

If I learned anything in light of recent events, it's the importance of never acting on impulse. Too bad for Nate, though. He should have contemplated the possible consequences of his actions before stealing a beer from Ole Man Keller, not to mention nabbing the rose bushes from the garden center in town, the bronze lawn ornaments in Fairview, and the crab pots and fuel from the workboats' gas tanks. And he certainly didn't think about his latest escapade of breaking and entering a home just to use the shower. Most importantly, he should have known better than to piss off residents in a small town where they live by their own rules and their own form of justice. The fallout from Nate's dreadful decision-making ultimately led to his jacked-up blue truck being sent to the bottom of Mine Creek. Nate himself was tied naked to the pilling at the county wharf as the tide slowly receded, leaving a sticky, salty residue over his body that invited every biting insect from Rumbley Harbor to dine on Nate's sunburned skin. His screaming horror echoed all the way across the water to Smithtown. Some say it was heard as far as New Jersey. It wasn't until the police department received an anonymous call did they retrieve Nate from the pier, and the torturous sound finally ended. A necklace made of fishing twine hung around his neck with a note scribbled in black marker, *"This is only a warning."*

With his skin sunbaked and covered in bug bite welts, Nate willingly accepted a police escort out of town. Hopefully, that would be the last time Nate would ever be seen or heard from again. Some say he got what he deserved, and there is a small part of me that agrees, but I'll defer judgment and leave that up to the big guy in the sky.

The doorbell rang and the dogs bounded for the front door. "Get back you two heathens, I got this." Hank brushed the dogs aside and turned the knob.

"Is Molly home?" A man my age stood on the step with a bouquet of mixed flowers filling his arms. Puzzled, Hank said, "Sure, come on in." He called out, "Molly, there is someone asking for you. Can you come in here now, please?"

The fragrant smell created a nauseous knee-jerk reaction. "Oh my god, Billy, no more flowers. I want nothing to do with them ever again." I said.

"What's this all about?" asked Hank, his voice swelling into agitation.

"I'm sorry Billy, it's okay. Thank you for bringing flowers, they're very pretty."

"Don't sweat it. I bet you're still a bit unnerved from everything that's happened to you. I just stopped by to make sure you are doing alright. Saw the whole story on television. Who knew the florist was this scary little dude? Spine-chilling when you think about it."

"I'm a little hung over from the Ketamine, whatever that is, but they said I will be back to normal by tomorrow."

"Oh yeah, I'm familiar with that drug. We deal with a lot of overdoses in my line of work. Ketamine is categorized as a dissociative anesthetic, usually used on animals. It can make you feel detached from your body and surroundings in a state sometimes referred to as conscious sedation. You're aware of what is happening to you, but unable to move or speak. It is especially dangerous when it is mixed with alcohol." Billy looked at me and I responded with an eye roll. "Sometimes it falls into the wrong hands and is used to incapacitate people for the purpose of sexual assaults. It's slipped into a beverage without a person knowing. That's probably what happened to you."

"Yes, he served a strange-tasting tea."

"You're lucky though. Too much of the stuff can potentially lead to fatal paralysis of the respiratory system. You experience a death similar to drowning. "

"Molly, who the hell is this guy?" Hank's eyebrows tightened into a confused knot, hoping for an explanation that made sense.

"I work at the County Morgue. Didn't Molly tell you about me?" Billy was innocently caught in the crossfire and started fidgeting with his collar. "We've been friends since we were kids, just lost track of each other until recently and because of Peters, I almost lost her again."

Hank shot me a look. "No, I'm afraid she failed to mention you."

"Hank, this is Billy Spicer, we grew up in the same neighborhood and went to the same school." I was careful not to dredge up the prom incident or the payback kiss at the morgue.

"Yeah, she sure was something back then. Still is. You are a fortunate man." He nodded to my husband, whose agitation was increasing by the second.

"Why don't you take Billy to the kitchen and make him some coffee," I said.

"Alright I can do that, but you just sit still and relax. You need to rest if you want to feel better. Remember, doctor's orders. Come on, Billy." Hank grumbled all the way to the kitchen with Billy following behind like a puppy. I took Hank's advice and plopped my aching body down in the lounger.

Another hard knock came on the front door. "What is this, a parade?" Hank continued grumbling all the way from the kitchen to the front door until he saw who it was. "Come on in Walt, I'm making coffee."

"With donuts?"

"Sure, why not? Let's have a party while we're at it."

"I came to see Molly. It's official business."

"She's all yours." Hank pointed to the lounge chair I occupied with elevated feet. "I'll let you know when the coffee is ready."

"Thanks, I'll be there in a bit. This won't take long." Walter removed his official sheriff's department-issued hat and hung it on the coat hook by the door then sat down next to me. "Feeling any better, Mol?" he asked. "Funny, it wasn't so long ago that I asked you that exact same question in this house."

I couldn't gauge his expression other than wrung out and somewhat relieved. "Seems like a lifetime ago to me."

"Yeah I guess so." He turned to look out the window, lost in thought.

It was true, in some ways I was different now. Permanently scarred from gaining wisdom I preferred not to own. I should have been satisfied this nightmare ended, but the disheartening truth was I could never return to the way I was before. Even though, in a way, I had released the woman from her watery grave, she will always be a part of me and will never fully vanish from my memory.

"We need to talk about a few matters. First of which being I have learned the hard way it's best not to leave you out of the loop, especially if it involves you on any level. Maybe in time when things settle down I can find a place for you in the office. Unofficially, that is. Sure would be better for my health."

"Wait, you mean us two working together? Ha, we wouldn't last three minutes and you know it."

"Yeah, you're probably right about that." Walter laughed and so did I, for the first time since the beginning of my involvement with Peters and this whole mess. I believe this was Walter's way of apologizing. Maybe we can come to some sort of understanding, maybe even develop a friendship, but that would be too much to expect at this point.

"Alright then, are you going to tell me why you're here or what?"

"If you give me a chance."

"Hank already told me they figured out the identity of that woman from the water. They connected the sandal to her, didn't they? Just like I said before, you should have listened to me."

"Yes, they did. Sandy Morrison's parents contacted the police and identified the shoe along with the tattoo on her body. Her parents are devastated from learning the truth about her secret life. She was a straight-A student. Cops searched her room and found her diary hidden inside a fake book, you know, the kind with the middle pages carved out. It was full of naked selfie pictures. You were right about Peters being the photographer; they were taken with his Polaroid camera. There were pictures of Sandy with Nate and Peters together. I can't get those images out of my head, poor girl. Sad, really, her room was still covered in pink flowered wallpaper with ribbons from the high school track team tacked to a cork board. Don't know how her parents will ever recover." Walter hung his head and anxiously rubbed his hands together.

"I don't think I ever will either." Tears welled up in my eyes. I let them roll freely down my face, each salty drop honoring Sandy's life and, at last, releasing her from the water.

"How did you find me at Peters' house? How did you know I was there?" I sniffled.

"Earl Leigh and I searched the backside of his house after he said he saw you go in the flower shop after hours."

"I was looking for a connection that would prove Peters' involvement and found a lot more than I was looking for."

"Yeah, you sure did. That picture of the Mayor took me by surprise. We had no idea how deep this went. The photo evidence is what they needed to help cinch the deal.

"Wait, did you just say you and Earl Leigh searched the house?"

"Yes. Earl Leigh was pretty fired up when he called me. He filled me in on Peters' past and it all started to fit together. Loud music was coming from inside the house. Peters was singing, real crazy like."

"I'm not sure I remember Earl Leigh there. Guess I owe him a thank you."

"Guess you owe me one as well."

"I am grateful to you both. I don't know where I'd be if…" my voice trailed off. I couldn't finish the thought.

"Aw, don't sweat it. You can have me over for supper sometime soon. Chops on the grill would be good, with grilled potatoes and green beans. Fresh beans, mind you, not the mushy canned green beans unless you make 'em in the oven with mushroom soup with the crunchy onions on top."

"Okay, it's a deal." I wondered which was going to be harder to pull off: maintaining civility with Walter or cooking a recognizable dinner.

"Did Hank tell you what we found in the greenhouse?"

"Yeah he did. That was a pretty gruesome finding."

"That's when I called in for back up."

"Hank told me you shot Peters in the ass."

"He was moving too fast, I couldn't get one off in his leg."

"Good thing you're a terrible shot, for Peters' sake." In spite of being drugged and held captive against my will, I still managed to keep my snarky edge.

"Ha, good thing you have a mean right hook. Must have been a hefty whack to knock him down."

"So what will happen to that jerk face now?"

"They searched Peters' vehicle for evidence and Sandy's other sandal was found. It must have fallen off when he shoved her inside the trunk. That was enough evidence to hit him with the additional homicide charge along with accomplice charges in sex and drug trafficking. I was included in the interrogation when he confessed to murdering Sandy Morrison. He said it was an accident and that he didn't mean to kill the Road Hawk's stable girl. He explained he mistakenly gave her too much Ketamine and she stopped breathing. He had every intention of returning her to the stable for another ride in the future. Like I explained before, there's no remorse for a psychopath."

"But he acted so normal."

"Yeah that's part of it. Smart enough to master the skill of deception. He used the death flower to cover up the decomposing body smells. Forensics is still running their tests but it's a safe guess the body part belongs to his ex-girlfriend."

"Oh, that awful cactus. He left one on my steps as his calling card." I shivered at the thought of Peters lining me up as the new member of the Dead Girls Club.

"Peters' basement was used as a drug warehouse. It spanned the entire length of the floral business. The whole place was chock-full of narcotics. Peters didn't care about the drugs, allowing their operation in exchange for his dates. The bastards are going down for a very very long time, every single Road Hawk and especially their head honcho."

"Oh yes, I met him. Scary dude."

"Where?"

"Rank's."

"Oh Molly, you have to stay away from there. They will eat you alive for a snack."

"Never again," I answered in all honesty. I never wanted to see the inside of that place again.

"I'll try and believe you."

"Tell me what else you know."

"Their operation went farther than originally thought, possibly supplying the tri state areas. I heard Peters is singing like a bluebird now, throwing everyone under the bus and turning state's evidence in exchange for housing in a lighter security facility. Go figure. He commits several homicides and ends up a guest in the state country club, the kind where they coddle the criminal who's who. You know those corrupt politicians and Hollywood types. The Criminal Justice System at its best, ironically not for the family of Sandy Morrison."

"I don't understand why the motorcycle clan didn't take care of Peters in their own way." I thought about Victor Handy ending up face down in the tidal ditch, and shuddered again.

"I don't think they knew he killed her because he had picked Sandy up at her home that night and not at the bar. Besides, they needed Peters for their grunt work. The little twerp was valuable."

Silence stretched between us like an invisible force field. In reality, I was only a frog's hair away from being the next victim and the thought pounded my head to dizziness. "What about the rest of the gang's stable girls? What happens to them now?"

"Rehab, I guess, or not, unfortunately. At least that little sick group is finished for now.

"My head hurts. I think I've had enough for one day."

"Listen, it's up to you how much you think Hank needs to know about your involvement in this matter." Walter stood up and waited for his sore knees to cooperate before going to join Hank in the kitchen.

"Oh, and there's one more thing. Here, this is for you." He smiled and handed me a piece of paper that was folded in half.

"What's this?"

"It's a summons for your court appearance."

"A court appearance? What for now?"

"Don't you remember? From when you rammed your van door into a vehicle at Walmart You're on the surveillance video. Does that ring your bell now? The guy immediately lodged a complaint against you. That's what you get for damaging a man's car on purpose."

"Aw, you know not. You got to be kidding me, after everything that's happened? This is ridiculous."

"All-righty then, time for a cup of coffee." Walter left me stewing in the recliner to join Hank and Billy in the kitchen.

"Thanks for nothing," I hollered out and closed my eyes, rubbing my aching head.

## - *Nineteen* -

Hank and I were finally alone. It only took several cups of coffee and two helpings of donuts to convince Billy and Walter that I was in safe hands. My overwrought husband, on the other hand, paced the floors of our house without one word for twenty painfully long minutes. The words left unspoken between the two of us were enough to fill Lake Erie. His heavy footsteps made the floor creak with each footfall. It felt like an eternity before he stopped and stood in front of the recliner, looking dead-on at me. I went too far this time and I knew it. My stomach ached.

"Hank, listen—"

"No."

"It was my fault and I know I deserve whatever punishment that comes my way but—"

"No Molly, you listen for once." Hank threw his hands in the air.

I had probably permanently screwed up any chance of getting into heaven and pushed my marriage to the point of no return. "Hon, listen to me, pretty please with gravy on top? I just wanted to help, that's all. You know I try hard to be a decent person, I really do, but it doesn't always work out that way."

"You're trying, alright. Trying to send me to an early grave. It's a good thing that I'm heavily insured because I don't think you could exist on your own."

"I promise I will do better from now on. I mean it this time."

"Seriously?" he snapped.

"Serious as a heart attack."

"Yeah right, if only that were true." Hank went silent before grinning at me. "Come on, honestly I would be disappointed if it was true. To tell you the truth, I'm proud of you, Molly. Most folks wouldn't have had the courage or chutzpah to help those women the way you did. What I'm trying to say here is I love you more than words can explain. But for my sake, you really need to cut this shit out."

Here I was thinking I was about to get the biggest ass-chewing of my life and this handsome man says he is proud of me? Maybe I was wrong about the way my luck rolls. If there is one thing I do know for sure it's that I am the luckiest woman to be alive right now and my husband loves me for who I am, not for who I thought I should be.

I couldn't love this man any more than I already do. I understand now that he loves me just as much. Without warning, a feeling rose from within me, one that was buried deep from somewhere I had once forgotten. I took in a deep breath of air filled with triumph. Just like that, at that very moment, I knew Smithtown would be okay again and piece itself back together. And so would I.

"Come here." Hank pulled me in close by my waist and kissed my lips in a way that sent tingles directly to my Hoo-ha.

And for me, that said it all.

## About the Author

**Michele M. Green** is a professional artist, musician and writer whose works are done plein air by foot, boat or canoe and as a result she has an intimate and personal relationship with nature and the landscape. She has been a frequent contributor to the Outdoor Delaware Magazine and her work is popular in many prominent collections including that of President Joe Biden.

Michele resides on an island with her husband and two dogs in the lower eastern shore of Maryland where she writes her Molly Hanson mystery novels.

You can contact Michele by email at:

greenbanjo@hotmail.com

## Acknowledgements

The Island Ran Red was printed in Palatino Linotype on an old crappy laptop with the letter Q cap missing from the keyboard.

Thank you Blueberry Lane Books for putting my book out there on the map, and to my editors Ben Parris and Chris Falchetti for your patience and generous guidance throughout the process. You are my Superheroes. Special thanks to Nicole Kosar for further editorial assistance.

And a huge thank you to my husband Buck, who never complains about my shenanigan side.

**Upcoming titles by Michele M. Green**

The Island Bruised Black

The Island Sold Out

The Island Fell Dark

The Island Played Dead

The Island Told Lies

The Island Stood Still

Made in the USA
Columbia, SC
17 May 2021

38116075R00145